Leaving Franny

A Dark River Crossing

Waldref Brant

authorHOUSE®

AuthorHouse™
1663 Liberty Drive
Bloomington, IN 47403
www.authorhouse.com
Phone: 1-800-839-8640

This book is a work of fiction. Names, characters, places, and incidents either are products of the author's imagination or are used fictitiously. Any resemblance to actual events or locales or persons, living or dead, is entirely coincidental.

First published by AuthorHouse 3/30/2010

ISBN: 978-1-4490-6587-4 (e)
ISBN: 978-1-4490-6588-1 (sc)
ISBN: 978-1-4490-6589-8 (hc)

Library of Congress Control Number: 2009913894

Printed in the United States of America
Bloomington, Indiana

This book is printed on acid-free paper.

Acknowledgments

To my friend Arlene Breckenridge, PhD, who took time from your busy schedule to proof my book. I appreciate your help, Arlene.

Thanks to my family and friends for their encouragement, especially my husband, Roger, who kept the coffee coming, strong and hot. Thanks, love.

Golf on friends!

Part One

Prologue

There are times when one's mind, through an overabundance of complacency, chooses to accept a condition, such as a sound or a smell, without recognizing it. It is as though it can become acceptable to our senses with such stealth that we are not aware of its existence. Then for some unknown reason we become conscious of it, and we are startled. For instance, a teakettle has boiled dry and is scorching on a hot burner while we sit a few feet away, reading the paper. The smell of the hot teakettle should alert us to turn the burner off, but something within us chooses to ignore it. Another instance would be a noise at the window. You're suddenly startled by it, but you know instinctively that it isn't a new sound, but one that has been there for a while.

So when did I first become aware of the smell that was making my blood run cold with fear? Was there some sense of it when I unlocked my car? When I leaned in to throw my junk into the passenger seat, was it there?

Had the boozy stench of someone's breath been there in the dark? Was someone there … watching me? Now I was paralyzed with something more than fear, it was terror. I heard my voice shout "God!" as though he had promised to watch my back, but had fallen asleep.

Before the sound of his name died on my lips, a hand shot out, grabbing the back of my hair, yanking my head back sharply. "Keep yer God damned mouth shut, er-al shut'er fer-ya!" a voice breathed close to my ear.

My memory went into overdrive. I had buried most of my past deep in my subconscious a while ago. I wanted it to stay buried forever, but now those deeply guarded secrets of mine roared back, taking control of my psyche ... No mercy!

The unvarnished truth reclaimed its place in my mind, and an indescribable loathing washed over me. I was plunged into the crushing memories of my sordid past.

Chapter 1

I remembered it all now, starting at the beginning. I had the misfortune of being born Frances Faye Beck, the oldest child in the extremely dysfunctional Beck family. There were five other family members: my mother, Mary; my father, Nick; Willard, the older of my two brothers; Charles, the youngest boy; and Sharon, fourteen years my junior, the youngest member of my family and the only one to live a normal life.

My family home was a hovel, built in a remote wooded valley miles away from the nearest human contact in Fenwick, a small North Dakota town. In this small community, my family was viewed as barely human by more conventional people. Our mysterious lives were fodder for many tales. Some were not true ... but most were.

There were countless rumors and unending speculation about our odd family, living in that secluded valley deep in the woods. There was a rumor, for instance, that my mother wrapped her thick grey hair up in a twist and affixed it to her head with rusty carpenter nails. Nothing warmed the hearts of the good people of Fenwick like a juicy rumor.

The funny thing is, my mother did wrap her hair in a twist and anchor it with nails. She used rusty nails because those were the nails she had access to, and because rusty nails didn't slip from her hair as readily as shiny ones.

The daughter of a prosperous farming family, my mother, Mary Lawrence, met and fell in love with my father, Nick Beck, a migrant farmhand, when he came up from Arkansas for the northern harvest.

It was no secret that my mother was a little slow mentally; she also became more and more eccentric as she aged, probably because of the situation she found herself and her children in. There were few conveniences at our disposal. We lived our lives longing simply for comfort and safety.

My father was a hard worker and physically strong; he was devious and cunning, but he was the type who was always down on his luck. Bad luck he generated himself with his irrational decisions and negative reaction to the constraints of civilized society. He drove an old beat-up Ford pickup that hardly ran and had no heater—but he owned a fine thoroughbred horse, a magnificent, high-strung creature that he kept in the stable and rode on rare occasions. To illustrate further: his home was not equipped with a telephone because he said he couldn't afford it, but his hobby was playing poker for real money.

He was a walking contradiction. He quoted passages from the Bible and lived by a code of ethics that would frighten even the most callous sinner. My brothers and I tried to stay out of his way. We learned early in life that we were nonpeople.

Nick's life of common labor and meager comforts was etched on his face. He arrived in the harvest fields of North Dakota having already lived a very hard life, a clandestine life kept in the strictest confidence between him and himself only. "Mind yer own business" was his only answer when questioned about his origins. "I come up from Arkansas, that's all ya need ta know," he would say, but when he removed his shirt on those hot August days in the fields, there were deep scars on his back and arms. Was it a sign of his past life, or an omen predicting our family's future?

If someone were to ask you what Nick looked like, you might say that he looked like Charles Manson. The biggest difference between the two of them was that Manson was almost diminutive, and Nick was huge. He looked as though he had fallen from Jack's beanstalk—lean and rawboned, with curly black hair dipping too close to his eyes. His eyes had the appearance of cunning and were too close together, deep-set and hooded, with bushy black brows.

It didn't take long before those dark eyes of his met those of pretty Mary Lawrence, my mother. He was attracted to her immediately. Pictures I saw of her when she was a girl showed her with brown hair, fair skin with freckles, and a broad smile.

I could readily see why he fell for her. She was lovely, well-groomed, and her freckled face with its broad smile betrayed an innocence that was very appealing. Her limited intellect and nonexistent experience led her his way. He was bigger than life to her. She was strangely drawn to him. She found herself thinking of him way too much. She felt guilty for thinking of his huge rawboned frame at night. His deep-set black eyes, hooded by thick brows, and his jet-black hair set him apart from anyone she had ever known.

She was a cloistered girl, in love with love. I have to believe that's the only explanation for her attraction to this man who was to become my father.

Chapter 2

Lunch for the field hands was always served picnic-style on the edge of whatever field they happened to be working that day. Blankets would be spread out in the shade, if there was any shade to be found. There was always an abundance of different foods served up, but there was one staple: fried chicken. That was handy because it could be eaten with the fingers, and it was easily transported to the field. There were also pickles, buns sliced and buttered, and green onions standing in a glass, like a bouquet. There was always a feast for the "hands."

The crew would sit around on the blankets, talking and laughing. It was a time to relax, to replenish tired bodies. My grandparents didn't believe in rushing through this meal. To them, it was a time to rejuvenate spiritually and physically. My grandfather Mathew always offered up prayers for the crew and for the harvest.

According to my grandmother Nina, Nick would station himself near my mother, striking up a conversation with her. It was usually a silly, lighthearted exchange between them, teasing and flirting.

Unfortunately, by the time the harvest was complete, Nick had decided that he wasn't going back to Arkansas without her. One day they simply stole away and were married by a justice of the peace. Nick moved into the big house and took charge of my mother's life.

There is a distinct possibility that the happy union three weeks earlier between my uncle Paul and his childhood sweetheart, Patricia Garvey, motivated my mother to consent to the clandestine union. She stood with Paul and Patty when they took their vows; they had made their wedding a very private affair, with just family and a few friends. Neither Patty nor Uncle Paul welcomed a lot of fanfare but preferred a quiet honeymoon hiking in the mountains near Coeur d'Alene, Idaho. Mary could have been inspired by that event, but there was one glaring difference between them: Patty was loved sincerely by Grandma Nina and Grandpa Mat. Nick was not.

Things would have been different if my grandparents could have controlled this situation, if they had been forewarned, but it was a stealth operation and, by the time they found out, it was done. Nick was by no means their choice. My grandmother was heartbroken, thinking of her daughter living with him and under his control, but there was nothing she could do now. They were already married.

Grandpa and Grandma Lawrence staked "the newlyweds" to a spread of land about eight miles from Fenwick, their generosity spurred by a burning desire to rid themselves of their new son-in-law and to keep their daughter from moving back to Arkansas with him. They thought this was one way they could keep her close enough for them to keep an eye on her.

My mother told me that Pops started building as soon as spring broke. The need for space between the new in-laws was mutually desired. "I can't stand yer ole man," he would complain to my mother. He pitched a tent in the middle of the building site and spent long hours every day working on his new house. At night, he would collapse on a cot he kept in the tent until work time in the morning. By the time harvest rolled around again, he had a livable house. Barely livable!

The newlyweds stayed with my grandparents just long enough to work the harvest and then, as soon as work was completed in the fall, they collected their pay and moved into their new house. It was built low under the trees like some haunted house that could have slipped from the pages of a horror story. Mother would never have told my father what she really thought of that house, because she would never have wanted to ridicule his handiwork and run the risk of hurting his feelings. She moved in because it was Nick's house, and she wanted to please him. It was a mistake, the first of many.

In all the years our family lived in that house, it was never painted. That was the place to which my mother came when she left the warm embrace of her loving family and began her heartbreaking journey. She had chosen a cruel life.

By the time I came along, their first baby, the freshness of the marriage had worn off, and my father put Mom to work. He told her that she would have to start pulling her own weight. Chuckling, he would remind her, "Yer lucky I took ya in, with yer bein' a numbskull and all." She wouldn't respond in kind but would absorb the comment in the good-natured way her natural gentleness dictated.

Her workload left her exhausted every evening. She cared for me, her firstborn, often carrying me on her back while she worked in the field or gathered in hay for the cattle in the winter. When I could walk, I would follow behind her in the fields and entertain myself while she worked.

She tended a huge garden, preserved fruit and vegetables for the winter table, and cared for the animals. In the evening, she would come in from her work exhausted and disheveled to prepare the evening meal. Nick would complain if she took too long clearing the dishes away and tending to evening chores. He would let her know that he expected more from her by yelling from their bed, "A man's ole lady should be in a man's bed not playin' around out there all night."

During the next five years, my brothers were born in that tiny shack. They would call it home for most of their childhood years. Some children are just born unlucky!

Chapter 3

Harvest time was about the only time there was any communication between my parents and my grandparents, other than the letters my grandma Nina and my mother regularly exchanged. My mother was never privileged to have postage stamps, but she would smuggle change to the mailman when she had enough put together for a stamp, and he would attach postage to her letters covertly.

She secretly lived for harvest time when she was alone with her family while Nick was in the fields. My grandparents savored the time spent with their daughter and grandchildren as well, but it always ended too soon and badly.

They would try to pry information out of my mother without seeming to interrogate her about her lot in life. They could see that she was not faring well. They would insinuate that there would always be a place for her and her children in their home. It was a promise that they never articulated, but it was definitely an invitation for her to leave him and come home.

Nick would hire on to work the harvest because the money was good. Always in need of money, he jumped at the chance to work. I can't think of too many things I admired about my father, but one thing he could do well was manual labor. He had the strength of two and would work from morning to night without complaint.

When he worked for my grandfather, he felt he had earned his pay many times over, because he was forced to put up with my mother visiting her family unsupervised while he worked in the field. Nick didn't want the crew from Arkansas to see her shouldering man's work, so he grudgingly let her stay inside to visit with her family.

Still another reason Mary wasn't expected to help in the fields when he worked for my grandparents was that he was still trying to prove that they were wrong about him, that he was somehow the best choice for their daughter. He made the ludicrous assumption that he could somehow change their opinion of him, or he probably just didn't want to get caught showing his abusive side. The certainty that he would not be employed by Mat Lawrence if he had any delusions that Mat's daughter would shoulder man's work surely figured into the equation.

Nick resented my grandfather Mat because he knew that he was barely tolerated by his father-in-law. The two men were polar opposites, and Nick was on the wrong end of the equation. Working as a farmhand for his wife's "ole man" galled him no end; he resented every word and every smile my mother and her parents exchanged. He suspected that she was talking about matters pertaining to the life they shared in the little house he had built. He warned her on many occasions that their lives were private and that she was not to share their private lives with anyone, including her parents.

"She's prob'ly in there runnin' her yap about me," he would growl. "Someday she'll learn to keep 'er mouth shut! I can't wait to git 'er otta here. Oh, she'll shut 'er Goddamned yap all right, er-al shut it fer her!"

The honeymoon was over.

I remember clearly the fear we all felt when it was time to leave my grandparents' home. I remember furtive glances made at his stony face. My mother would try to sidetrack his anger with pathetic attempts to chat lightheartedly about the day and the recipes she had gotten from her mother, but we all knew Mom was probably going to be beaten. Maybe we were all going to be beaten, who knew? I prayed that was all.

The abuse we had become accustomed to was escalating from occasional to constant, hard-core physical, mental, and emotional abuse. Nick became more inventive at creating punishments as time passed. He began ranting incoherently to justify his behavior. He would site visions of Jesus appearing to him, commanding him not to "spare the rod" in order to save us from ourselves.

It was as though all the powers in the universe were at his disposal, and we were the ungrateful recipients of his magnificent edicts. "Ya know why I had-ta do this," he would admonish us. "I knew you'd make me do it." Then he would prophesy, "Jesus told me ta watch ya. He told me ta keep an eye on ya." After he had taken his fill of whatever cruel perversion he wanted to indulge himself in, he would charge, "Now look whatcha made me do!"

Things were constantly getting worse for us. It was not safe where we lived. We were all in constant fear. I don't think there has ever been a man more feared than Pops was ... or more hated.

My mother prized an old hutch that her mother had given her. It reminded her of her family and the wonderful life they had provided for her. It was a nice old piece of furniture, the only one she owned. She would run her hand over the smooth surface of the hutch, remembering her mother and the home that she had left. It would comfort her in a way, until she remembered that stashed behind it was the cattle whip soaked with her blood and the blood of her children.

Any imagined slight, disrespectful glance, or neglected chore could trigger a flesh-ripping session with that awful weapon. A whipping usually drew blood and was, more times than not, the prelude to some heinous humiliation after the first passion of rage was worn out.

For instance, you might be beaten bloody and then put into solitary confinement for a few days or a week and sometimes more, depending on the infraction you were charged with, or how petulant dear Father felt at the time you were banished. Rations were meager when you were in solitary, and humiliating confessions and other degrading acts were required of you to get them.

When you got solitary confinement, you were locked in an old boxcar that Pops had confiscated from the junkyard, originally for the purpose of storing grain at harvest time. It was easily converted to the dual purpose of housing convicted family members, just by adding a lock to the door. Simple!

When the "box" was full of grain, he would use his alternate chamber, a hole under the shack that was meant for use as a cellar for storing foodstuffs. Like the "box," it had a dual purpose. The cellar was accessed by pulling a square piece of the floor away, exposing a ladder that ran down the mud wall to the mud floor.

The ladder also had a dual purpose. Old Pops was handy that way. An offender could be tied to that ladder in a standing position for a few days. That would get your attention. You were also vulnerable to many other little twists while hanging there ... whatever the "dear one" deemed appropriate.

My brothers were the recipients of this penalty more than I, but none of us were immune to being dragged into these horrible places. I remember the inside of these ugly dark places all too vividly. I was dragged there usually for a different reason.

Punishment was not always a whipping and then some form of reasoned finale. Sometimes it was spontaneous and meted out instantaneously with fist, boot, or knee, but it was always accompanied by the incoherent ranting and accusations of that mentally unbalanced pervert.

A back torn open by a cattle whip would always be preferred to a black eye or broken nose, for obvious reasons. My brothers and I attended school and were often in the public eye. We always hid our wounds; we were not allowed to disclose family business. It was against the rules.

We were taught early in life that nothing went beyond the four walls of our house, and I was grateful for that. I was glad no one knew about me or about my unspeakable secret. I knew instinctively at a very young age that the darkest of evils was forced on me by my father, and I was besieged with guilt and revulsion.

I have no idea when the molestation began. It was before I had the ability to reason or remember. I only know that I could not remember a time in my life when I didn't know the taste of my father's semen.

When I was younger, he would hold my shoulders, shaking me for emphasis after these obscene acts. "Ya keep yer trap shut now er al throw ya out and the Gypsies'll git-cha. Ya don't want that! They love ta catch little girls." Then he would pat my cheek. "Good girl, now git oter here."

Later, when I was older, he used a perverse form of reverse psychology, and he would threaten me by saying, "I'll tell yer Mama an' she won't love ya anymore, that's fer sure!"

I would beg him, "Please, Pops, please don't tell Mama."

When I was older, he would choke me or hit me and threaten, "Open yer Goddamn yap and I'll shut'r fer ya ... fer good!" He was especially nasty when he was drunk. He was a nasty, smelly, brutal old drunk, and I despised his filthy existence.

I lived in fear of the beatings and that my secret would be exposed. I had a recurring dream that my father was dead, wonderful dreams that I dreamed both asleep and awake. If he were dead I could forget the cold, dark box and the struggle not to swallow until it was safe to spit ... I could be good ... and my mouth would be clean.

Chapter 4

There came a time when my father began spending occasional nights away from home. He was becoming known as a high roller at some of the dives in the city, gambling away the grocery money and laughing it up. "I own this game," he would brag. Gambling did fit him well, and he excelled at it. None of the proceeds were wasted on the needs of his family; they were spent to advance his image as a big spending gambling man, the king of the dives.

Nobody crossed my father. He was proud of the hold he had on his gambling friends in these places. They knew he was boss. If a fight broke out or someone got out of line, he would pound the man senseless. Simple! When a game ended badly for him, though, he came home ready to deliver a message from Jesus. We didn't stand a chance.

I could imagine him there with his friends, drinking, whoring, cursing, and gambling. Laughing his big toothy laugh … Bastard! He could spew his paranoid garbage, and other equally drunk and paranoid losers were always sympathetic. Just what he needed—someone to encourage him.

He could never have imagined how much his family lived for those times when he was away from home. It was a joyous occasion, a time for silly jubilation. It was a time for frantic self-expression, for throwing things and yelling, for silly talk and laughter.

All too soon it would end. We would hear his old pickup rattling down the drive, and the joy we felt gave way to the familiar feeling of fear and loathing. When he came home, he was usually drunk or had a hangover. He was a mean drunk, so he was always looking for trouble. He would stride through the house and outbuildings eyeing everything, searching for the inevitable infraction, evidence that someone needed to be "straightened out." We all feared him, and I despised him as well.

I was always singled out to compromise myself in order to preserve my safety, always pretending to smile while my belly tossed with fear. *Die, you bastard! Die!*

Resentment toward me was building among my brothers and even my mother, because I seemed to engender some coy perverted flirtatiousness in my father. He would say things like, "Come and sit on yer old Pops' knee, purdy girl." My skin would crawl, but I was afraid not to go to him. I would have to smile and obey. Because of these times, I seemed to be favored by him; the rest of the family suspected me of snitching on them or something.

Sometimes I was tricked by the old pervert into disclosing secrets, or sometimes I would snitch because I wanted to escape his wrath and turn it to someone else. It wasn't that I was exempt from any of Pops' wrath, but it was more that he would talk as though we were confidants. He took pleasure in pitting the rest of the family against me for some perverse reason, often calling me "my Franny."

He enjoyed the cold looks I was lavished with at these times. He probably felt popular, as though we were competing for his affection in some way, because of my mother's and two brothers' reaction to his destructive foolishness.

The cold reception I received from my mother and siblings left me more isolated than any of them could have imagined. I was cut off from the rest of the family, and I feared and hated my father. I longed for the approval of my family, especially my mom, and I lived life with a foreboding of impending horror that never left me.

I can't forget the time Char's father brought her with him when he came to see Pops for some business arrangement they had. Char was my friend from school; while the two men were talking, she ran into the house to see me. It was after a particularly bad incident in which my mother suffered under Pops' whip.

Her hair was disheveled and her shirt was beginning to soak up the blood from the wounds on her back and arms. Char had no sooner entered our house when my poor mother, still crazed by the ordeal, reached behind the old hutch and produced Pops' whip. She thrust it in Char's face, blood and all. "This is what he uses on us," she hissed. Then glaring at me, "And you can tell your old son-of-a-bitch that I told her," she said.

Char's face went white, her eyes fixed on the bloody thing, unable to digest what she had just heard. She just stood there slack-jawed, looking horrified. I grabbed her arm and pulled her outside. "Don't pay any attention to Mom," I said. "It's not true, she's just mad at him."

Little by little, my mother began to morph into the peculiar eccentric that people found so entertaining. Few people even remembered the modest young woman who was a little bit slow. Her face reflected the results of life with an abuser. She was worn and leathery; the life force had left her eyes.

She always wore a dress over denim pants. It was the kind of dress that women wore generations before her. It fell just above her ankles. Over it, she wore an apron like the one her grandmother must have worn. Most of her shopping was conducted at garage sales; that including shopping for her wardrobe.

She seldom spoke and had few friends—no friends, really, except for her mother. The woman she had become wore men's work shoes on her feet and rusty nails in her prematurely gray hair; she was suspicious of everyone, including me. I longed for my mother, but I no longer knew this woman.

Chapter 5

Now thirteen years old and in the final grade of the tiny school we had all attended, I was an okay student, all things considered, but not a favorite with most of the girls in my school. I dressed funny, in odd homemade clothes, and probably smelled a little as well.

Each day my brothers and I would arrive at the little school in Noble, a tiny little town outside Fenwick, driving a horse-drawn wagon like those you read about in history class, while the rest of the world traveled in automobiles. The school bus didn't service our address because we were the only family living in the area with school-age children. We lived at the very end of a remote road. The costs of bus service to our area could not be justified for just one family, so it wasn't included in the route.

In the wintertime, we would drive a horse-drawn sleigh, even during the coldest winter weather. This was the only transportation to and from school that my father would afford us. There was one worn-out old Ford pickup in the family, and it was my father's exclusively.

We would arrive at the school half-frozen, bundled in hand-me-down clothes with blankets and bricks that my mother heated in the oven to keep our hands and feet from freezing. Our hair was always crumpled and tousled from winter hats and scarves, and our noses were always runny from the cold. Some students took delight in ridiculing us. "Your nose, your nose, where icicles grows," they would chant.

Life was difficult for us, but in spite of everything, this was the best of our world. We felt safe when we were in school, the one place where he couldn't get us. We loved being there. Thinking back, though, we were never completely safe from Pops' orneriness, even when we were in school. I remember one instance when Willie opened his lunch bag and found that Pops had substituted a bloody turkey's head for his lunch.

This was humor? The man truly was disturbed, and he wasn't getting any better. I'm sure he found it very satisfying to know that Willie was hungry, satisfying to know that life for Willie was always one wound after another, bruise on bruise! He had become Pops' main target, the preferred receptacle for our father's rage and the first one to be chosen for "discipline."

I, on the other hand, was the receptacle for his brutal filth. I was being destroyed from within. I hated to go home after school, but I was afraid to tell anyone; if they knew, they wouldn't like me anymore, and Pops would find out that I told!

On days when the thermometer would dip too low, Hugh Brody, our teacher, would wait by the door in the entryway and motion to us with a jerk of his head. "Follow me, children," he would say as he escorted us into the basement, where there were three chairs set up by a huge furnace radiating a tremendous amount of heat.

"Take your wraps off, everyone, and I'll get something warm for you." He would disappear up the stairs and, in a few minutes, return with a cup of hot chocolate, or tea loaded with sugar, for each of us. "When you're warm, come up and we'll begin."

Mr. Brody was the only employee of the school. The school was his, and he was an excellent caretaker. He taught grades one through eight. His school was one large square building. It was divided into two parts, with the teacher's quarters on one side of the building and the classroom, a large cloakroom, and a separate entry with a bell tower in the other part.

In spite of the small number of students, everyone referred to him by his proper name, Mr. Brody, never by his first name, Hugh. All thirty-three students loved him, and he returned their love. We were his family. It was a privilege I would always treasure, and I hold him in my prayers even now.

He would assign special duties to those who earned them by doing a good job with their schoolwork, or sometimes they would win a contest or get the highest score on a test.

One such special duty was to ring the bell in the morning for the start of the school day and again to signify when lunchtime was over. The other special duty was to gather the chalkboard erasers, take them out of doors, and pound the chalk from them on the side of the stucco building. Mr. Brody told us to pound them on the side that couldn't be seen from the road.

It was an honor to be chosen for either of these jobs, especially the bell ringing, and students competed for them through spelling, math, and history contests. For the lower grades, there were coloring and reading contests. There was always a competition of one kind or another for different prizes and honors.

Mr. Brody always made learning interesting and fun, but the jewel that shined the brightest was the Christmas program. The school would be decorated to the extreme. Tinsel, ornaments, and bells were hung all over. The front of the schoolroom was cordoned off and sheets hung to fashion a make-do stage for the dazzling performances that were to be presented there. Rehearsals and singing practices abounded; the excitement was almost more than we children could bear. Mr. Brody would play the piano, and the kids would sing carols. Tinsel rustled, carols rose, laughter rang out, and there was warmth all over the place.

Hugh Brody knew how to stimulate enthusiasm. He was the pied piper!

Chapter 6

Charlene Wellston was my friend during school hours, but nothing beyond that. Our parents didn't spend time together, and we lived miles apart. The Wellston family had very little in common with my family, but Char and her brother Ben always befriended me and my two brothers.

There was an occasional visit to conduct business pertaining to gathering crops or other farm topics between our parents, but never a personal friendship between the two families. This was true of all the neighbors in the community. We were never guests at anyone's home.

I was envious of kids who talked about adventures they had together after school or during vacation. I dreamed of being popular, of having lots of friends. Char was my closest friend, and sometimes I would go to the Wellstons' with Pops when he needed to talk to Vernon about some farming business. Pops often rented land from Vernon Wellston for grazing cattle during the summer, since we had a very small farm and needed additional land for grazing.

The Wellston family had a dog that they had named Pup. I thought that was a very strange name. To me, it sounded as if they could never decide on a name for the dog. On those occasions when Pops went to the Wellstons' farm to discuss business, Pup would react strongly to him. Hair standing on end and teeth bared, he would hold Pops at bay and refuse to let him step from his old Ford pickup.

Vernon Wellston would restrain the dog by holding his collar. He always apologized for his dog's reaction, but secretly he probably didn't mind that much. Pops was not a favored visitor at the Wellstons', but still it was strange Pup reacted so violently to him. Maybe the dog could sense how cruel and sinful my father was. *Sic him! Sic him!* I would silently urge.

Pup wasn't the only member of the Wellston family who was uncomfortable around my father. Helena Wellston, Char's mom, hated to be in the same room with him and felt that he leered at her. She often said that she thought he was evil, and he was overbearing and conniving. "He has satanic eyes," she said. "And he's loud and obnoxious."

He was never forgiven for spitting a huge wad of chewing tobacco into her fireplace, but that couldn't compare to her total disdain for him because of his treatment of his two boys. Char and I overheard a conversation between Char's parent about my father concerning an incident involving Willie and Chucky. Neither of her parents realized we were within ear shot of the conversation, they thought we had left the house. It was during a particularly cold spell one winter evening. Pops had left the boys sitting in his old pickup for hours while he sat inside sipping coffee and talking to Vernon. I had been allowed to come in and play with Char, but the boys were left outside. When Helena insisted that they come in and get warm, he refused, saying, "They can stay out there. They're tough."

After Pops left the house she told Vernon to conduct business with him outside from that point on, and not to invite him into the house.

"You're just upset about the spitting, Helena," Vernon teased.

Helena slammed the cupboard shut. "Well, he sure as hell knows better than to leave those boys in that leaky old rattle-trap for hours, with no heat, while he warms his own rotten old ass in here by the fire. Just keep him away from me!"

"Okay, simmer down now," Vernon said.

"There's something very wrong going on over there," she said. "I think he's molesting that little girl too, Vern. I just have a very bad feeling about him." I asked Char what was meant by the word "molesting" but she didn't know either.

"My God, Helena! Do you hear what you're saying? You can't accuse a man of something like that! Now that's enough!"

"Mark my words, old man, there's something very wrong there. Mary should get rid of that son-of-a-bitch!" She went on, "I don't trust that old fool!"

Helena could never have imagined the true extent of his evil. She always felt sorry for my mother and reached out to her on those rare occasions when my mother attended a school function or some event that would bring them together.

Chapter 7

Char and I talked endlessly about the Christmas program. We practiced our lines and practiced playing the musical instruments. I was cast in the part of an angel. I was ecstatic. Imagine me, an angel! My good fortune was beyond belief.

Another good thing about playing the part of an angel was that the costume was kept, from year to year, and it would be provided for me. I didn't have to try to convince my parents to supply it. I knew it would have been a disaster if I tried to get a costume from them, and now that worry was taken away. It was too good to be true. This was my best Christmas ever!

On the day before the Christmas program, Char asked, "What time will you be here, Franny? Please come early. My mom is bringing food, and she said we would be here by one o'clock so she can get everything ready, and guess what—we can go into Mr. Brody's place and help her. I don't think anybody has been in there. Have you been in there, Franny?"

"No, I've been downstairs but not in his place," I told her. Suddenly, Char reached out and squeezed my hand. "You're the best friend I ever had, Char," I told her. "I hope we will be friends forever."

"Forever and ever!" she answered.

The day before the Christmas program, we were all out of our minds with excitement, and Mr. Brody wisely decided to use the entire day for last-minute decorating and practicing our lines. I felt the peace of Christmas for the first time in my life. I opened myself to the preparations at hand.

Pops was going to be gone on one of his two-day junkets to Fargo, so there would be true peace on earth, for a while anyway. He wasn't interested in the school program and said he wouldn't be back to attend it. He had never attended a school function that I could remember, so peace would reign for this wonderful day. Merry Christmas!

I was up early the day of the Christmas program. I had my breakfast, laid my clothes out, and prepared my bathwater. This was not an easy chore, although it did seem a little easier on this special day. First, water had to be heated on the primitive old wood-burning stove. I completed my chores while my water was heating, my excitement motivating me. I bathed and washed my hair, and then I dressed carefully and fixed my hair. I was happy when Willie told me timidly that he thought I was pretty, because I wanted to look especially nice since I was to be the Christmas angel.

It was still too early to leave for the school, so I sat and waited for what seemed to be an eternity while my mother and brothers were getting ready to leave. I could barely wait to join my friend Char and her mother in Mr. Brody's quarters and to recite my lines and sing the carols we had practiced.

Finally, it was time to go to the school. We loaded the sled with blankets to cover our legs, heated bricks for our feet, and a hot dish my mother had prepared for the party.

We were fortunate that the Christmas program had been planned for early in the afternoon when the temperature would reach the day's highs.

I didn't want to mess my hair up by wearing a hat and wrapping my face with my scarf, but it was probably going to be necessary, especially later, on the way home. Winters were cold in North Dakota.

It was turning out to be a wonderful sunny day with barely a breeze. The temperature had risen throughout the day, one of those rare winter days with the water dripping here and there as the ice melts, and when you speak, you can hear a slight echo in the clear blue atmosphere.

We settled into the sled with the blanket over our knees, me with no hat. Maybe I could get to the school without messy hair after all. Willie slapped the reigns on the horse's back. "Get up" he said, and we were off.

When we turned off the driveway onto the road, Pops was waiting there in his old truck. "Git out, Franny; yer stayin' home with me," he said.

"No! I'm in the program. I'm the Christmas angel," I yelled in desperation. I looked frantically at my mother for help. Her face was frozen, unreadable, and she said nothing. She looked away while he pulled me from the sleigh, abandoned, completely alone, and filled with loathing. He threw me in his old truck.

I felt my heart break in my chest. *Please,* I thought, *just let me have this one thing, one memory that I can think about later without shame!*

The level of revulsion I felt for him has never been equaled in my lifetime. Hearing this ugly, smelly old man telling me to "be a good girl, yer gunna fergit all about that ole program" was more than I could endure.

My fear now took second place to my need to have my good memory, to stop being a nonperson. Then it was blunted even more by complete and utter loathing, and it brought me to a very dangerous place that I no longer controlled but observed from outside my body.

I surrendered completely, for the first time, to the thing that I would come to recognize later as the monster within me, a malignant abyss of unreasoning, pure, black hatred. *Fight or flight? I guess I will start with flight, and if that doesn't work, I'll try to fight. God help me!*

"I hate you," I hissed and, yanking the door open, I fell out of the old pickup as it skidded to a gravel-plowing halt. I scrambled to my feet and ran away from the road toward the wooded pasture. Into the brambles I went, my nice Christmas outfit snagging and tearing. I looked frantically around myself for somewhere to go. A place to hide from the dirty bastard!

I heard good old Pops bellowing, "Don't make me come fer ya; ya don't want that, come on now and al go easy." I crawled under a clump of tall dried broom grass that had blown over, making a sort of a hollow shelter where the snow had drifted over it. I held my breath, hoping that some miracle would save me—but sadly, it did not.

Pops' big boots presented themselves to me quietly. They just stepped into my line of vision and stopped. It was the calm before the storm. I was well aware of that. I silently cursed the boots and the man in them to hell, and I hoped that it burned hot for him!

"Git up otta there now," he said, his voice low with rage. I slowly started crawling out, and he lifted me the rest of the way by my hair. I could smell his boozy breath, and I knew he was drunk. Pops was a mean drunk, and I knew this would not end well. I was no physical match for him.

He lifted me by my waistband and the hair on the back of my head and carried me to the old truck. Throwing me across the driver's seat into the passenger side, he climbed in behind me and struck me in my mouth with the back of his fist. I turned my face away from him and, in one motion, he grabbed the hair on the back of my head again. Driving with his left hand, he pulled my head back hard with his right hand so that I was unable to move and everything looked blurry.

I sort of surrendered myself to the inevitable. I knew what the outcome would be. I could taste the blood from my split lip, warm and salty.

When we got to the house, Pops slammed the old truck to a screeching halt. He slammed the door open and, before the truck stopped rolling, he stepped out, dragging me across the driver's side seat behind him as you would an old jacket. Without breaking his grip on my hair, without waiting for the truck to stop rolling, and without closing the truck door, he hauled me to the house.

Once there, he threw me through the door and exacted the retribution he needed for my rejection of him. It seemed as though time had stopped; me and my monster sat by, watched it unfold, but we didn't contribute.

Neither begging nor cries of pain were given him, just the blackest hatred ever known to man, denying him his prize. Giving him no response, no utterance. The punishment went on unabated as he tried to elicit his fruit. We both saw it all. He failed.

He must have been convinced finally that he had mortally wounded me, because he abruptly stopped his busy work and meekly stole away saying that I had forced him to do this. "Now look what-cha made me do," he lamented. I heard him shuffle his way up the stairs. I listened to see if he would return, but after some time I heard him snore, and I knew he was through … for today.

"Die, you dirty bastard, die!" I whispered. I lay on the kitchen floor covered with broken glass, cream, and blood. Clumps of my long black hair lay beside me. I felt as though I hardly existed, tiny and dirty and all used up. My monster was sleeping now, too. The only part of me that was still awake was my self-loathing. It consumed me. There was no Christmas angel here.

Chapter 8

I don't know how long I lay naked and bleeding on the floor, but my mother and my brothers eventually came home. They stood inside the kitchen door in silence, staring at me.

I didn't look at them. I lay on my side, my eyes fixed on the horizon of the kitchen floor. I saw the rubble, the broken glass, the hair, the blood, the cream, the dull patches on the worn old linoleum floor where the glossy finish had worn away, and I saw their shoes and beyond that the open door. Cold winter air pushed through the open door and washed over me.

There was no hope anymore. There was a time when I thought maybe I would escape this place ... but no more, no more!

I could feel my mother's eyes on me now, and I resented it. I didn't look back. I didn't love her anymore. She had gone to the Christmas program and left me behind. She knew, and she didn't care. She left me there. Alone! I wanted her to see the damage she had permitted him to do. I wanted to see her weep and beg for my forgiveness, so I could have the privilege of denying her, the privilege to be cold and indifferent and say, "Take your stupid face and look away!"

Mom gently touched my shoulder; I recoiled from her touch, but when she whispered my name I could resist no longer. My need was so great, and I was so weak. I was without pride or self-respect, so I accepted her pretence of love and resisted no longer.

She gently lifted my body and held me in her arms. It was the first time in a very long time that she had held me. I didn't want her to make me love her again, but I couldn't resist. Mom held me in her arms. None of it mattered. Who else would pretend to love me, if not her?

She told Willie and Chuck to change their clothes and attend to their chores. Willie was crying softly. He wiped his nose on the back of his hand as he walked away. Once they had gone, she told me that she had talked with Helena Wellston about everything, and that Helena was going to try to help us.

"Helena told me that it is my duty to report Pops to the authorities," Mom said. "She told me that if I don't report it, she will, and if she does, Pops and I will probably both go to jail." I felt the antagonism I held for Mom soften a little. "We'll do something about this, Franny," she whispered. "Next time he leaves, we'll sneak out and go for help. Don't tell the boys, though; if he finds out, he'll kill us both. As soon as you feel good, we go!"

I didn't trust my mother. I still held the image in my mind of her turning her stony face away from me as he dragged me from the sleigh. I didn't really believe I would ever be able to leave this place. I couldn't let myself believe in life again. "Mom," I said, "Just let me lay down for a while."

Later, I told her about the attack and the way Pops had dragged me to the house and thrown me inside. The way I tried to get away by throwing a chair in front of him as I ran. How he had tripped over it, falling to the floor. Then even more furious than before, how he had thrown a jar filled with cream that was sitting on the table. It hit me, breaking the jar and knocking me to the floor.

The way I had refused to give him anything. Showing no fear, no cries of pain, no begging, and I told her how desperate he had been for that. I told her that I was dragged, thrown, and kicked around in the cream and broken glass, my body serving as a mop of sorts, but I still didn't give him anything.

I didn't tell her that I had only observed the beating from a safe place or how the monster living inside me sat with me and watched, too. I knew she wouldn't understand, and I wasn't sure I did yet either. "He told me that I caused it, and I had to clean it up. That's why he dragged me all around in it. He used my hair for a mop. He told me, 'Yer gonna burn in hell, Franny!' I thought he was gonna kill me, Mom," I said, and added, "He probably will someday."

Fortunately, there were two weeks of Christmas vacation from school. That gave me time to partially recover from my injuries, at least enough to go back to school. My bruises were fading, and I had a slight limp, but life went on as usual. Unfortunately.

During the first week back in school, Mr. Brody gave me a note for my parents. "Make sure your mother gets this," he said. "I'll be checking to see whether she got it or not." I was worried. Mr. Brody usually didn't threaten to check on my honesty. I knew this had to be something bad. How could this be? Was it some report about me or one of my brothers? I debated whether I should discard it or deliver it, but in the end I decided I should do the right thing. I brought it home unopened and gave it to my mother. That was the safest bet.

When she saw the note, she looked at it for a moment, and then her eyes found mine. A look passed between us. I had no idea what it meant, but I would soon find out.

Unknown to me, the note was a decoy to enable my mother and I to leave the house without Pops---long enough for Helena Wellston to spirit us off to go to the police in Fargo. It said that there was to be a meeting at the school to discuss several issues regarding changes in the school curriculum and the possibility that a nurse would visit the school to administer immunization shots that all schoolchildren were required to have. Knowing that Pops would refuse to attend any school function or meeting, Mom placed the note on the table in front of him unopened. He opened it, read it, and tossed it in front of her. "This is yers," he said. That was her green light, an excuse to get away from home without him for an afternoon. Later, when Mom explained to me what had just transpired, my heart stopped in my chest. Could we get away with this?

It seemed a lifetime dragged by before the moment arrived for our attempt to escape. Why does the hope of acquiring that which you yearn for most, but are least certain to attain, bring with it such misery? One would think that hope alone would ease the burden of unhappiness, but it's the burden of endless hoping that's the torture. Add time to the equation to tantalize you with endless longing for its quick passage, and it's the worst of all tortures. It can hardly be resisted.

Our plan was to use the pretence of attending a parent-teacher meeting to meet with Helena Wellston at the school. She would drive us to the police station in Fargo, where we would report my father and persuade the police to arrest him.

We both knew that if we were not successful in convincing the police to arrest him immediately, we could not return home. If we did, we would probably both disappear and never be found alive. I worried that, in the end, my mother would not have the nerve to follow through with her plan.

You can't ever know what unspeakable courage it takes to defy your abuser unless you've been abused. After you taste the bitter surrender of your will to the force of an abuser, you lose the part of you that instinctively strives for freedom, and you become compliant. Taking a stand against one's abuser is almost impossible. I couldn't bring myself to believe that my mother was up to the task. I held the memory of her voice in my mind, pleading and groveling, as we all had, under his cruel hand—but I, on the other hand, had bested him recently, denied him his prize. I was strengthened by that.

On the fateful night of the Christmas program, when my mother had spoken with Helena about our problem, Helena had proposed a plan to attempt an escape. The problem was that coordinating an escape was virtually impossible, because we didn't have a means of communicating. We weren't allowed to own a telephone, so we were isolated.

All the stars in the heavens would have to be aligned if we hoped to make this plan work. I was excited and afraid, and I knew my mother had to be just as fearful. If he suspected that we were trying to go to the police … God help us! He would, factually, beat us to death. He always demanded that nothing left the four walls of our house, and that was not negotiable. This was a desperate action, and we were desperate people.

In a sad and quirky turn of events, my father had errands to run the day of the "school meeting," and out of an overabundance of generosity he offered to give us a lift to the meeting. He would drop us off at the school and return to pick us up in an hour or two.

We immediately thought Pops suspected that something wasn't quite right. He always had to control everything; maybe that's what motivated him to drive us. Still, we were afraid he might have talked with one of the neighbors who had children in the school and found out that they hadn't received a notice from Mr. Brody to attend a school meeting. We were both scared to death that he had caught us in a lie.

So the plan was aborted, and we spent the time we had managed to steal talking with Mr. Brody and Helena, planning possible ways to handle a future escape in such a way that no one would get hurt. We also considered the evidence we should present to ensure Nick's immediate incarceration. It was obvious that we would not be safe if we were ever alone with him after we reported him to the police.

The whole conversation was very difficult for me. I was humiliated knowing my teacher and Char's mom were both aware of this nasty part of my life. I also felt guilty for telling family secrets, when the rule had always been not to tell anything about the family. Mr. Brody and Helena were both stunned by our story. They could not predict whether the police would physically haul him away or not, but they both agreed that we couldn't continue life as we had been living it.

"Surely if you tell the police your story and also that you are not safe to be alone with him, they will arrest him without forewarning him in order to protect your family," Helena said. I was amazed that civilized people cared about us and were willing to help us. Amazing!

Mr. Brody looked from face to face. "We must be very clever here; we mustn't endanger you more than you already are. Secrecy is most important. No one can know," he said, looking at me pointedly.

"I'm not telling!" I said. I felt defensive. I was a champion when it came to keeping nasty secrets!

"You could all be in grave danger if we make a mistake. Someone could lose their … or, well, could really get hurt, so when Nick comes we will tell him that I wanted to discuss immunization shots for you children. The shots are required, and I don't believe any of you have them. So there you have it; we will tell him that this is why I called you down today. Agreed?"

Mr. Brody looked worried, and I noticed the gray strands in his red hair. His clear blue eyes were magnified through his thick lenses. My heart swelled as I listened to his voice and saw his kind imperfect face. "Mr. Brody, do you think we should tell a lie?" I asked.

"Desperate times call for desperate measures, so yes, we should lie this time. I'll talk to you about that later," he answered. "We must put a plan in place before he returns or … What?" he asked.

"He's here," I told Mr. Brody.

"He's here? Okay, Franny." He looked into my eyes. "Don't you give up, and no talking!" He pressed my hand briefly.

Mr. Brody walked to the wretched old pickup with us and engaged my father in conversation, talking about immunization shots for my brothers and me and how they were a requirement. "Not many takers fer yer meetin'," my father said.

"Most students have their immunization shots," Mr. Brody retorted with a smile.

"I spoze," Pops answered with a big toothy grin. I couldn't detect any tension, and I relaxed as much as I could with Pops in the picture. The two of them exchanged some pleasant small talk, and we were off. The ride home was silent and uneventful. Life at the Becks was unchanged.

The failure of our plan to escape crushed me. Hopelessness washed over me like never before. There was no relief; life went on and on and on. Thoughts of suicide plagued me constantly.

Chapter 9

It can't be stated too many times that Pops bore a striking resemblance to Charles Manson. His raving, his Biblical quotes, and his crazy predictions bore more than a little similarity to the evil old convict. I think we all realized that Pops might be criminally insane and seemed to be spiraling deeper and deeper into his dark, evil delusions.

I didn't know exactly what happened to set Pops off this particular time, but I could hear my name, and I knew I had to be at least part of the problem. Willie was the oldest of my brothers and had often found himself on the receiving end of dear old Pops' rage. I think the old man may have been envious of Willie. It occurred to me that in his evil, twisted, delusional haze, he thought of Willie as his competition—that I had rejected him because I preferred Willie—and therefore, he had to be vanquished.

He launched a criminal attack on Willie the likes of which not even we, his family, had witnessed before. It was as though he wanted him dead. We all stood transfixed in horror, but none of us had the courage to come to my brother's aid. I could hear Willie beg, "Please Pops, let me put my shirt on first."

After the sadistic attack, still holding his trusty old bloodstained whip, his fists bloodied from beating Willie, good old

Pops dragged his son out into the snow. I could see the steam rolling off the wounds on Willie's back and head, freezing and floating above him. Hoisting Willie along by one arm, as the boy's knees buckled with every step, unable to support his own weight, Pops threw Willie's shirtless, battered body into his frozen chamber of horrors, with orders that all food and drink be withheld from him. He slid the heavy door shut and locked it, leaving Willie shirtless in the dark box to bleed and shiver in the freezing cold.

It was winter, and we all knew Willie could not survive long where he was. The weather was warming slowly and water sometimes dripped during the warmest part of the day where the sun warmed a sheltered nook, but at night the thermometer dropped well below freezing temperatures, sometimes below zero. The box was insulated; it held the winter's cold long after the weather warmed up in the spring, and it definitely wasn't warm yet. Willie wouldn't survive for long in it, especially in his condition.

Pops sat there drinking his beer and staring into the night, savoring his handiwork, his eyes attached to the boxcar. It was as though he was afraid Willie would somehow pick himself off the floor like a phoenix rising from its ashes, break down the heavy door, and escape into the night.

After what seemed to be hours of tossing, I must have fallen asleep, because I was awakened by my mother with a hand over my mouth. "Be quiet," she whispered. "We're going tonight, get up!"

I followed her out of the house, and we silently closed the door. She handed me my clothes, coat, hat, scarf, gloves, and boots. Our escape had finally started for real.

"Do you think we woke him?" I asked.

"We … naaa, I think he's drunk," she waved. I snorted my disapproval.

A sense of urgency drove us, because we knew if we were not successful this time, Willie would die for sure, and we would probably die as well. "He has the keys to the pickup in his pocket, we're going to have to walk," she said. "It doesn't matter; I can't drive the truck anyway, so let's just go."

"We'll never make it, Mom, we have to cross the river, and I think it's open in places."

"We have no choice. Come on, we're going to have to run as far as we can, just in case."

We ran until we couldn't run any more, until my lungs were exploding, and still we were not at the river. It was dark, and the branches of the trees and underbrush clawed our skin and gouged into our flesh. "Keep going. We have to make it before dawn, or he'll be up and after us," Mom prodded. We ran like wild things through the night, scaring up birds and wildlife as we crashed through the brush. Finally we arrived at the river. We were exhausted, and we were afraid that we had taken too much time.

"Thank God it is frozen over, we can run across," I said, but I was worried.

"We need to find a long stick, Franny," Mom said. "Come help me find one." We frantically looked for a long branch and finally located an aspen sapling that my mother thought would do. It was about three inches in diameter and fifteen or more feet long. We struggled together to break it free and get it to the bank of the river. Once there, we slid it out on the shiny black ice. "Now get down on the ice and inch your way out slowly, but don't let go of the stick, rest part of your weight on the stick. You hear me?" she said.

"All right," I nodded, getting down on the ice. I knew she was feeling nervous about this crossing, and I didn't trust the depth of the ice either. The water was swift in this part of the river; it had a tendency to wash away the ice from the underside in places. "It'll be fine," I said, but I was concerned. I inched my way across the ice, feeling it flex and bow down under my weight. I remembered that my brothers and I used to call it rubber ice.

The ice held for me, and finally I was across the river looking back at my mother. She made a fist and held it up in victory. "Yes!" I had to get the aspen branch back to my mother, so I gave it a mighty shove. It skittered across the shiny black snowless ice and stopped just short of the bank.

Mom lay down on the ice and inched her way toward the stick. Closer and closer until she could reach her hand out and pull the slender log to her. She began inching her way across the thin rubbery ice, her arm locked around the stick, pushing the stick with her as she went. The ice was bending too much under her weight.

"Mom, put more of your weight on the stick!" I yelled.

"I'm trying to," she said.

"Well, hurry!" I yelled. Then the unthinkable happened, and the river made a little puddle where she lay. The ice wasn't holding, and water was leaking from somewhere, pooling around her body. "Mom!" I screamed. "Hurry up!"

Slowly, her feet and legs began to sink and become submerged beneath the surface. She desperately pushed the stick, kicking frantically, water and ice flying everywhere. I threw myself down and slithered over the icy dark surface toward her. Grabbing the stick, I pulled as hard as I could, but I was slipping on the snowless ice. *I can't let her go*, I thought, as I anxiously clung to every slippery thing and soon joined Mom in the icy water of the mighty Mouse River.

I was surprised to find that, as I thrashed around, I could touch the bottom. The icy water felt like needles piercing my skin, but it was only waist deep. We were standing on the bottom of the river, but the ice was all around us. I was losing my strength, and I could hardly hold the stick that we had carried with us out onto the ice. My mother and I stood looking at each other. The futility of our mission smothered us.

We were soaked and freezing. "It's too late to turn back, Franny, we move on," she said, and she stepped around me and began to break the thin ice, moving forward step by step. All those years of brutal work and little comfort had taken a lot away from my mother, but it had made her tough, and that's what was needed in this situation. She had no intention of failing Willie or failing me … this time. Now this weird eccentric woman was teaching me about courage. I was proud of her!

We fought on, breaking the ice and moving forward and finally, close to the edge where the ice was thicker, we were able to pull ourselves up and onto the ice, with the help of our stick. We reached the bank of the river and climbed out. Our clothes were freezing, and I could hardly feel my arms, legs, or feet.

"We have to keep moving or we won't make it, so I want you to move as fast as you can," she said. "We'll go upriver to Ernie Cranston's place; he might give us a lift. We'll never make Fargo walking. We'll freeze." We pushed on along the river and then cut across where the river made a bend and doubled back on itself. Finally we heard dogs barking in the night as we approached.

Chapter 10

The dogs were frenzied and crazy. I was afraid of them and clung to my mother, holding her between me and the wildly barking dogs. The yard light came on, and Ernie Cranston appeared in the doorway. He hailed from London, England, and spoke with a thick British accent.

The strong floodlight mounted high on an electrical pole seemed to pull the color away from his face. He looked very light and grey. Everything around him looked grey and seemed to be suspended in time. Silence enveloped me, and I realized I was fainting. I grabbed for Mom, but I missed and went to my knees. I stayed for a while like that until the world was colored again. No one noticed what had happened. My mother thought I had tripped. She simply grabbed my collar and hoisted me up. Her eyes locked on the man in the doorway.

"Sorry to wake you, Ernie," Mom said. "We need your help!"

"Who's there?" he asked.

"Just me and Franny here," she said, pointing to her chest and then at me.

"Mother of God, what happened to you?" He took her shoulder, guiding her inside. "Come in, come inside," he said. "Do you know what time it is? Would you like to get Nick on the tele?" he asked.

"Tele?" she asked.

"Telephone," he told her.

"No, we don't have one. Ernie, we really need help, we need the police," she sobbed. "Could you take us into Fargo?" Mom asked him.

Ernie stood looking at us for a moment, confused. He wondered how best to handle the situation. Then finally, he said, "I'll get my coat. Would you like to call the bobbies before we go?"

"Call the bobbies? I guess I don't know who they are, bobbies? I don't know them," my mother answered.

"I'm sorry, Mrs. Beck. I should have said, do you want to call the police? I'll ring them for you if you like."

"Oh, I remember now, my parents called them bobbies, too. What should I tell 'em?" she asked.

"Well … just … tell them that you have a problem, and you would like their help. Tell them what your problem is," he coached. "I'm sure they will ask questions, so I don't think you'll have any trouble letting them know what you need. I have no experience with the police, but they'll help you along, I'm sure."

"All right, could you dial them?" Mom asked.

Ernie dialed the number and handed the telephone to my mother. "There you are, Mrs. Beck," he said.

"Hello," she yelled. "Oh, it's ringing," she told Ernie. "Yes, hello!" she yelled. "Just a minute, they want my name," she told Ernie.

"Oh, well, just go ahead and give it to them then," he said.

"I'm Mary Beck," she yelled. "They want to know what they can do for me," she whispered.

"Yes, well, just tell them then," he said.

"Well, all right, my husband beat my son, Willie Beck, so bad ... I don't know if he's alive." Her voice broke. "I think he is, but I want you to help me save him. He's locked in a box outside, and he's going to freeze. He doesn't have a shirt on or anything," she cried. "They want my address," she whispered.

"Just tell them that we are on our way to the station now, and we'll be there shortly," he instructed.

"We're on our way to the station, and we'll be there short-ly," she yelled and gave the phone to Ernie.

"Hello," he said. "Yes ... it should be about half an hour give or take ... You bet! Thank you!"

Could this be real? I thought. *It looks real. It looks as though we are going to go to the police and tell our story. The police will take their squad cars, drive down the dirt road that leads to our family home, slip the cuffs on good old Pops' wrists, then they will drag Pops away, and we will never hear from him again.* I felt tears of joy well up in my eyes, and I cried softly as we drove down Ernie's driveway and turned onto the highway.

My mother and I were thawing and dripping. I could smell the odor of our wet shoes, clothes, and hair—and not a nice scent, either. We were still shivering and cold because our clothes were wet. I could hear the fan on the car heater turned on high, but it didn't seem to make any difference.

Indeed, we felt better than we had while slogging along the mighty Mouse, but still we were cold to the bone, and we needed to be dry. Tears still streamed down my face, my teeth chattered, and I cried silently as anticipation and relief swept over me, wave after wave.

Unable to contain his curiosity any longer, Ernie finally broke his silence. After a few peeks in the rearview mirror, he cleared his throat. "You folks had some trouble?" he said into the rearview mirror.

"Yeah, we did," my mother answered.

"The young man, is he all right?" he asked the mirror.

"No," my mother said. Her sobbing stopped the conversation, and we all fell silent.

We drove in silence until we reached the police station. Ernie stopped as close as he could to the big glass doors, and we climbed out of the car.

"I'll park it and be right in," Ernie said.

The cold night air struck our wet bodies like a freight train. We clamored up the cold cement stairs. When that big glass door swung open and the warm air hit me, it was almost as though the universe had wrapped its arms around me and said, "Welcome!"

We stepped inside and started to make our way to the front desk. A hush fell over the place, and all eyes were on us. It occurred to me that we were probably the most pathetic-looking duo who had ever ventured into the station. I raised my hands and looked at them. They were covered with scratches from the branches and ice we had battled, and they oozed blood. I understood all too well why people were staring at us. I looked back and saw Ernie behind us, hat in hand. "Thank you," I mouthed.

"My pleasure," he nodded.

I will never understand why I felt so heartsick and guilty as my mother and I wove the web that would entrap Pops. I can only say that the jubilation I had felt earlier had completely reversed itself. The sheer ecstasy of exacting revenge on him had given way to self-doubt.

Did I cause him to do these things, as he said I had? I wondered if it could be true. I couldn't remember the first time it happened. Am I the one who caused it? I felt sick and nauseated. What about Willie? I will never forget his pleading, "Please, Pops, let me put my shirt on first!" If I hadn't tried to fight Pops, would Willie be in the box now? Willie had been beaten many times before, but this time was not like any other time ... did I do this? I wondered, *is he still alive? What have I done?* I had never felt such crushing guilt before.

We told the officers about Willie and how they would find him in the old boxcar, maybe alive, maybe not. We begged them not to wait for morning to rescue him, because he could already be dead, even now.

My mother told me to sit with Ernie while she talked with the officer. When I looked back at the two of them, the officer was looking at me, but he dropped his eyes when I looked back. I knew my secret was out. I felt ashamed; nausea swept over me again. I closed my eyes and swallowed. It seemed that this ordeal would never end.

Chapter 11

Finally, the officers were convinced and started organizing a squad to storm our farm and arrest my father. They asked that we go with them to point out where Willie was and to identify Pops. A caravan of three patrol cars wound its way down the old dirt road. My mother and I were in the lead car with one officer; another car followed us with three officers, and a third with two officers followed behind. Ernie followed behind all of them and turned off when he reached the gravel driveway that led to his house.

It was a sight to behold when we arrived at the farm. All those patrol cars with lights flashing illuminated the unpainted buildings and the boxcar. The red lights made the buildings and trees look surreal and desolate.

I saw the policemen moving slowly toward the house, resting their hands on their holsters. I was so overcome with guilt and fear that I tumbled out of the car and ran toward the house. "Pops," I sobbed, "I'm sorry!"

Fortunately, before I reached the house, one of the officers grabbed my arm. "Get back in the car!" he ordered. He pulled me back to the car, chucked me into the patrol car by my arm, and slammed the door behind me. Once there, my mother shot me a look that immobilized me. The officer crossed to her side of the car and tapped on the glass.

She rolled the window down and before he could speak, she said, "I'll keep her in here, but you better be ready, he's going to fight."

"Where is the boy?" the officer asked.

"He's in that boxcar over there."

"And it's locked?" he asked.

"Yeah, the key is inside. I think he's got it," she said, jerking her head toward the house.

"He's in the bedroom upstairs, you say?"

"Yes, up the steps and to your left."

"Okay, we'll get him," he said.

"Careful!" she answered.

He nodded and, touching his brim, joined the rest of the men waiting for him. After checking the back of the house, they all moved to the door. All but one of the officers filed into the house. The one left behind stood guard over the patrol car where we sat. I heard loud voices but no shots—that was an encouraging sign. It seemed like hours before they reappeared with Pops. His hands were cuffed behind his back, and his pockets were turned inside out.

He was a pathetic figure as they led him out of the house that he had built as a newlywed. There was a gash on his forehead, and his lip was bloody. His eyes darted around wildly and, when they found my mother and me, they locked themselves on us in a silent curse.

One of the officers held the keys above his head and rattled them as if to say, "We have them." We both scrambled from the car and hurried to the boxcar. We stood there, clutching each other, while the officer finally found the right key, unlocked the door, and slid it open.

"Hello," he called, his voice floating out in a cloud of frozen vapor. Taking his flashlight out of his belt, he pointed it around inside the boxcar. "I'll take a look," he said as he hopped up and disappeared into the darkness.

Moments later, he reappeared. "We'll need to get Rescue out here," he said. "Let's get him inside, and get Rescue on the fucking radio right now!" he said, nodding to one of the policemen. Then, turning to my mother, he asked, "Could you get some blankets, Mrs. Beck? Bring a couple please." He spoke in a monotone voice, trying to sound calm.

When they brought Willie in, he was wrapped in the blankets my mother had given them. They laid him gently down on the couch in our tiny sitting room. I could feel the cold radiating from his body. He struggled to sit up and failed. I thought he looked like a little old man. He was blue and shaking uncontrollably. His face was beaten bloody, unrecognizable; even his hair was matted with blood.

"I'm sorry he did this to you," I said. He didn't answer but feebly extended his hand to me, and I took it. Every breath had a small sound to it. I wondered if something inside him was broken, and if he could be mended. We sat like that while we waited for the ambulance, my mother and the police officers trying to warm Willie with blankets heated in the oven and a hot water bottle that Mom filled.

The ambulance arrived with more colored lights scampering from blue spruce to white pine tree and onto the buildings in rapid succession. The trees appeared black when the red colored light overlaid the green of the leaves, then white lights would scamper behind them, turning them green again. It was a bizarre sight, frolicking colors darting this way and that.

The rescue squad carried Willie out on a stretcher and carefully loaded him into the ambulance. He tried to resist being put into the ambulance, to no avail. "It's going to be all right, son," the officer said. "We have you now! We'll get you all fixed up."

We told Willie we would come and see him as soon as we could and waved goodbye. We knew that Willie probably couldn't hear us, but we said it anyway. The ambulance pulled up the driveway and onto the road. Once it disappeared, we turned, and there was Chuck. His face was white, and he looked very small. I put my arm around his shoulder. Mom and I looked at each other, expressionless. We were both empty.

It seemed to me that the night we ran through the woods and crossed the half-frozen river was eons ago. I raised my hands again and looked at them. The blood and scratches were still there. *It wasn't that long ago*, I thought. As irony would have it, my mother, sensing and probably wanting to blunt the enormity of what we had just done, whipped out a kettle and started to cook something. "Franny," she said, "I think I'm pregnant."

I was stunned. *How dare you be pregnant now, right in the middle of all of this? Yes!* I thought, *that would be about right. We need one more thing to worry about!* "Now you're pregnant?" I asked.

"Yup," she said, "I think I am. I guess I'll have to wait and see after everything that happened tonight; who knows, I probably am. I've seen worse!"

God! This can't be happening. I was beginning to go into overload, so I decided to choke it back, forget it, and store it with all the other appalling, unthinkable crap that I had in my mind and try not to think about. *I'm almost out of space,* I thought. I said, "What are you making, Mom?"

"I guess I don't know, Franny," she said. "That makes two things I am not sure about."

"Maybe we should just go to bed," I suggested.

"I'm tired," Chucky said, still looking pale and owl-eyed.

"Yup, we'll all go to bed, but I don't think I'll sleep much! So if you change your mind and you want something to eat … just ask me … I'll get up," she said.

I looked out the kitchen window and saw the first gleaming of morning's light on the horizon. Morning was dawning, and this was the first day of our emancipation. Sleep was impossible. Snippets of our daring escape played over and over in my mind. The stare Pops attached to my mother and me made me cringe. The way Willie looked when the officer fished him out of the boxcar. The way we had fallen into the swirling, ice-cold waters of the mighty Mouse River. The dogs barking wildly in the night and the uncontrollable fear I had of the dogs for some reason. The tightly guarded secrets my mother told the policemen. The sight of Pops led away in cuffs, by the police. The cold, gray, never-ending doubt and guilt I felt then … always. The red-hot sting of unbridled shame, there was no joy in it!

I remembered when I was tiny, how my mother would comfort me when things were bad, and I longed for her comfort once again. I got out of bed and went to her. "Could you make something to eat, Mom?" I asked.

"Good idea, honey, I thought you'd never ask," she said and climbed out of bed. I felt better just knowing she was awake. In truth, we needed to talk, my mother and I. We needed to rehash the events of the life-changing step we had taken.

Mom pulled out her kettle, heated it, and broke some eggs in it. "Slice some bread," she said, "we need some toast, too." Then, in one of those rare moments that you remember forever, she looked at me with a tiny twinkle in her eyes and said, "We did it!" A smile that I will never forget spread across her face. Some of her teeth were missing, testimony to the hard life she had been forced to lead. "We did it!" she said and held her arms open to me. I ran in.

We talked through the morning about how we had achieved the unachievable and where we might go from here. We vowed to each other that if the police didn't keep Pops in jail, we would have to do whatever we could to be safe. No matter what! One thing was perfectly clear to us: we couldn't exist in a world with him in it, should he be freed. Someone would die, and we planned for it not to be us. I was too young to comprehend the full meaning of our promise to each other, but I couldn't avoid taking on another layer of guilt for having made it.

Chuck woke up and shuffled into the kitchen. Mom turned to him and said, "You hungry, Chucky?"

"Do we have any bacon, Mom?"

"Yup," she said, "we do." To me, she said, "Go on, Franny, go lie down before you fall down."

"All right," I said, grateful for the invitation. I was exhausted. I washed up a little and went to bed. My head barely hit the pillow when I felt my spirit starting to float away from my body a little, and then nothing. No dreams ... no dreams!

Part Two

Chapter 12

When we woke, it was almost noon. We realized we had a problem if we were going to see Willie today. None of us was a licensed driver, and we needed to go on the interstate highway to get into Fargo. Chuck suggested that we practice driving. Then, when we had it down, we could slip under the radar undetected to see Willie. "Just drive on the driveway until you know how to steer, Mom." It was apparent that Chuck wanted to see his brother.

She looked at him with skepticism. "You think so, heh?"

"Yup, you drove the tractor, and it isn't that much different. Just get in there and drive it."

"I suppose you're right, Chucky," she said, hugging his head to her hip, "but we have to do our chores before we do anything else." We spent our early afternoon taking care of our regular morning duties, unhurried and relaxed, glancing at one another occasionally to confirm that it was all okay. After doing our daily routine, we bathed and dressed for the day and then turned our attention to the journey into Fargo. A daunting task, even though it was less than a twenty-mile trip.

Mom turned the key in the old jalopy, and away it went. "So far, so good!" she said. She pushed the clutch in but had no idea where to put the shift lever. "I need to back up. What one should I put it in?"

"R means reverse, Mom," Chuck said.

"R?"

"Yup, R."

She put the shift in the R position and looked back as though she was going to back up, but nothing happened.

"Mom, you have to let the pedal go and push on the gas now."

"I know, but I'm afraid." The truck started inching backward for a few feet and then slammed to a stop. "I can't do this!" she said. She turned the truck off and climbed out with the key in her hand. "That's it!" she said. We turned to walk to the house and, right on cue, Ernie came driving up the dirt road.

"I thought you might want to go in and see your boy today," he said. "I'll be happy to drive you, if that meets with your approval."

"Oh, thank you very much, Ernie, I could sure use a lift right now!"

"I thought you could … it would be a pleasure on my part. A nice drive sounds splendid. I should think you might want to check with the police, just to see what's going on with Nick as well?"

"That would be good of you, Ernie, if you don't mind," Mary said.

"I don't mean to insert myself into your private family business, but is your young man doing all right now?" he asked.

"I hope so, Ernie. We'll see. I'll let you know after I see him."

Once at St. Joseph Hospital in Fargo, we checked at the information desk and got Willie's room number. We were allowed to go in right away. Ernie stayed back and waited for us because he thought his presence might make Willie uncomfortable, since he was only a casual acquaintance. Willie was lying on his side with pillows all around him. His back, hands, and feet were bandaged. His face was cleaned up, but it was unrecognizable because of the swelling, lacerations, and contusions. His eyes were mere slits, and he had a cast on one arm and a brace on his neck.

"Can I get out of here?" he mumbled with his thick, swollen lips.

"You have to wait until the doctor says so, son."

"Where's Pops?"

"We'll talk, Willie."

"Mom, where's Pops?" he groaned. We told Willie about the night before and the arrest. We were shocked to see that he wasn't overjoyed at all, but seemed sort of heartbroken when we told him how we had slogged through the woods and crossed the half-frozen river to reported Pops to the police. We expected his undying gratitude for saving his life. What we got was no response from the slits where once his eyes were. "The cops?" he asked through his broken face, catching and holding me in his gaze. I dropped my eyes. I felt the guilt I was harboring rise, and my anger rose in response … a festering anger that I could hardly control.

Willie wanted to hear no more and turned his face to the wall. I saw his body convulse as he wept. Our new peace had its very first fissure, and it was less than one day old.

We waited for a while, glancing at one another nervously, and then left quietly. "We'll come and see you as soon as we can, Willie," Mom called. He didn't answer. I felt my cheeks pulsate; I was filled with anger.

We left the hospital, and Ernie drove us directly to the police station. I didn't hear what either of them said on the short journey. I stared out the side window watching the pavement slide under us, trying to tame the beast within me. Ernie let us off at the front steps. Once again, we made our way up the steps, through the big glass doors and up to the front desk. I glanced around; I had the uneasy feeling that Pops might be peering at me from some hidden nook. Ernie followed a short distance behind us, hat in hand, but instead of staying in the background, this time he approached the officer behind the desk.

"Good afternoon! This is Mrs. Nick Beck, Mary, and her daughter, Frances. They were told to report here today to complete and sign forms that you were preparing."

"Oh, yes. Mrs. Beck, just complete these forms and be sure to include all the information highlighted in yellow and your telephone number," the clerk behind the desk said, handing the forms through an opening in the glass barrier window that separated her from the public.

"Thank you, but I don't have a telephone," Mary said, pushing the papers back toward the clerk.

"No problem, Mary, give them my number. I'll come and get you if you need the tele."

"I don't want to impose on you, Ernie."

"It's no problem. It's my pleasure, Mary." He consoled her, resting his hand on her shoulder. I saw tears well up and glisten behind her lashes. "It's okay, Mary," he said gently. "Things will improve … I promise you."

We finished our business and left the police station. On the drive home, Ernie stopped at Gimbals Truck Stop and bought a hamburger for Chuck and me while Mom and he had the special of the day. We had never been treated to hamburgers before, and they were delightful. I devoured mine without talking to anyone. It was late, and I was famished. My anger melted away, and I felt comfortable and safe.

Another peaceful night passed without incident. It felt good. I wondered if I would ever be like my friends in school and do fun things whenever I pleased. Having fun and eating burgers whenever I wanted them. What a dream!

It was the beginning of March, and the weather was getting warmer every day. During the day, the sun shone warm on the frozen ground, and water would run everywhere. At night, things would freeze again. The dirt road leading to our farm was not good because grooves were forming in the melting ice that would catch your tires and hold you hostage, tossing you to and fro as you drove along in the frozen ruts. We completed our chores and were eating our lunch when Ernie came tossing up the road. There was a telephone call, and the date for the hearing had been set. My mother left with Ernie to call the court-appointed attorney who had been provided for her.

Chuck and I stayed behind and finished our lunch. We cleared the dishes away and finished our chores in the barn and tended to the cattle. We fed and brushed Pops' horse.

We were always afraid of that horse. He was big and jumpy, but we finished currying him and covered him with a horse blanket. Pops always wanted to make sure his horse was well cared for, but rarely gave his family the same consideration. I felt angry and spiteful. *I hate your dirty, damned horse*, I thought, *and I hate you, Pops!*

When we finished outside, Mom was already at home and busy making an oven dish for dinner. She motioned toward a newspaper on the table. I picked it up, and Mom pointed to an article with her paring knife.

LOCAL MAN ARRESTED FOR ASSAULT AND INCEST.

Nicholas Beck of Fenwick, North Dakota, was arrested early Friday morning. He is charged with assault with intent to do bodily harm and incest. Beck's son, who is presently in good condition at St. Joseph Hospital, was brutally attacked Thursday evening. Beck, who exhibited an extreme state of agitation, is scheduled for a mental competency evaluation to determine his fitness to stand trial. According to Beck's confession it is believed that he routinely abused all family members. April is targeted for Beck's arraignment.

"Mom, what is incest?"

Chapter 13

Ernie, whom we had scarcely known before the great escape, became a lynchpin in our survival. He was always helping us when we needed to go into Fargo for some reason or needed groceries or advice or were in need of his phone. He was always there, steady and refined. We all learned to love him.

Today, Ernie was going to help us bring Willie home from the hospital finally. "I wonder if Willie will be in a snit again today?" I said, feeling a little angry.

"Who knows?" Mom rolled her eyes "If he is, we leave him there," she laughed.

Chuck was outraged by that comment. "We're bringing Willie home today! He's my friend, and he can come home if he wants to. You should've brought him home the very next day," he yelled, frowning at us. "He's the man, not you!"

"The doctor said he had to stay, Chucky, until he got well. Don't worry; we'll let him come home today, okay?" Mom asked.

When we reached the hospital, we were greeted by a nurse pushing Willie into the waiting room in a wheelchair, his hands still bandaged and his cast and neck brace still in place. The swelling in his face had gone down somewhat, and his eyes were now visible. Beside him was a paper bag with his belongings in it, and the blankets we had sent with him were folded on his lap. The blankets looked old and dingy in these surroundings.

I was embarrassed and followed Mom, looking at the floor without speaking. It seemed to me that people in the hospital were staring at us. I resented it, and I felt my anger rising again. "Ready to go home, Willie?" Mom asked.

"I guess," he said without looking at her. It seemed to me that he could barely bring himself to answer her.

"Where in the hell would you rather go, Willie?" I hissed, trying not to let anyone hear me. "Can you tell me that? Because if you want to go somewhere else, just go! Just go! But don't you dare blame me for everything, and just go to hell!" Willie raised his eyes and looked at me. His eyes were profoundly sad, as though his heart was breaking.

"Folks! Folks! Let's try to treat each other with civility," Ernie said. I felt tears sting my eyes. *Everyone hates me*, I thought. *I hate you, Ernie. I hate all of you!* I was stung by Ernie's rebuff.

The nurse pushed Willie out of the hospital and over to Ernie's waiting car. I flung myself into the back seat and slammed the door behind me. I stared at the pavement through the side window and said nothing. *Everyone is helping Willie*, I thought. *No one has ever helped me when I needed it. Mom could have, but she didn't, she didn't help me at all. The best thing that ever happened to me was when Pops went to jail, and now Willie blames me! Thank God I have no father now. Thank God! And to hell with you, Willie!* The thought barely formulated itself in my mind when I felt a stab of conscience.

It wasn't earth-shattering, just an uneasy feeling in my stomach. "Not really, God," I said silently.

I should be feeling really happy, but Mom and Willie are both making me miserable, I thought. *Mom makes me mad when she hesitates and fumbles for words as if she hasn't got a clue, and Willie mopes over Pops like he was some kind of hero. Well, to hell with both of them,* I thought. "Sorry again, God, I didn't mean it!"

The feelings of isolation, anger, and guilt couldn't be healed simply by changing the situation in which I lived. I was learning that you could be all alone in a crowd. I was disappointed that I was still miserable even though we were rid of Pops. I had thought that everything would be wonderful when he was gone.

Ernie drove us home from the hospital. There was conversation, but I didn't really hear it because I was lost deep in those hurtful thoughts that wouldn't let me go.

In the weeks that followed, we were able to attain a more traditional family dynamic as we worked our way through assigning a pecking order to our fractured little group.

We let our guard down a little more each day and began to trust one another. We enjoyed quiet times, we had pleasant conversations, and it was nice.

We were fighting and making up, cursing one another and accusing each other of the precise things we knew would hurt the most, but miraculously through it all we began to heal. Willie and I grew closer once we were not under duress from Pops. He often held me if I was afraid or saddened by our plight, and I would hug him if I thought he was feeling bad. He kissed my hair sometimes instead of saying good morning. I loved that. There was no fear of showing kindness now that Pops was gone.

Willie and I were having one of our knockdown, dragout screaming matches when the caseworker from the county pulled up in her quiet blue car. Spotting her when she turned into our driveway, we stopped yelling at each other and scrambled around the kitchen trying to tidy up before she reached the door.

I could hardly believe my ears when she told my mother that she wanted to talk with Francis Beck. *My God,* I thought, *what does she want of me?*

She was a tall woman with glasses, and she carried a brown leather briefcase. It was flat and long and zipped on the top and sides. It was sleek, and so was she. She had a polished appearance, with her briefcase under her arm and her black pumps. "Hello, Mrs. Beck," she said. "My name is Lucille Adams. I'm your caseworker from the county. I wonder if I might talk with Francis in private for a moment." There was no end to the probing questions and clever way she extorted answers for them. I was uneasy and getting more uneasy as time went on. It seemed to me that I was unable to control myself, and answers flowed out of me uncensored. Things that I had kept secret from my only friend and even my family for so long fell out of my mouth uncontrolled. Finally, the guilt and lack of control made me feel desperate, and I could feel tears sting my eyes.

"You've done very well. You couldn't have prevented this, Frances. None of it was your fault. We'll talk again before the trial, but the worst is over. Things are going to be better for you from now on. I will have a little talk with Willie now,

72

and then I must head back to Fargo. Could you ask him if he will step in and sit with me for a minute?"

"Willie, she wants to see you now," I said. Willie looked at me like I was an apparition.

"Me? I don't have a fuckin' thing to say to her or anyone else about anything!"

"Well, Willie, she wants to see you," I said and took a chair at the table by Mom. Willie looked at both of us with a frantic expression, but in the end reluctantly took his turn in the tiny sitting room with Lucille Adams, the caseworker.

"Just tell the truth, Willie," Mom called after him.

I knew the questions the caseworker would ask him, and I knew it would be difficult for him to give an account of the abuse he had suffered at Pops' hands. I hoped he would find the courage and the good sense to tell the truth and get it over with. It was well over an hour before Willie reappeared from the sitting room. I looked at him, trying to see if he too had been brought to tears, but I could see no evidence of that. Mrs. Adams followed with her briefcase, looking cool and in control.

"Thank you all for your time. It was nice talking with you. We'll talk again soon. I don't think I'll talk with Charles this time. If we need to talk to him later, we'll let you know," she said. "As a matter of fact, I would have called before I came this time, but we are required to do a look-in without calling from time to time ... and of course, you don't have a telephone, so that, too."

My mother walked Mrs. Adams to her car and talked for a short time. We heard her give Lucille Adams Ernie's number for any future visits that were necessary.

Willie and I were bewildered by the visit and sat silently until the big blue car started easing its way up the driveway.

"Man, I wish I had a car like that!" Willie said.

"Me too," I answered.

Chapter 14

The snow and ice finally gave way to warm weather and turned the world into one huge mud puddle. "I hate this mud," my mother complained, cleaning away the mud overflowing the rug in front of the door. *Mud puddles,* I thought. *We have bigger worries than mud puddles,* and the first thing that came to my mind was the trial.

Suppose something went wrong at the trial and Pops would not be put away for a long, long time as we had hoped, but would instead be "rehabilitated" and sent home. *If they free him,* I thought, *Mom, Willie, and I are dead. That's all there is to that.* The possibility that my father's case would be dismissed caused me many sleepless nights, worrying and wondering.

I was having recurring nightmares that I would go to the mailbox to pick up the mail and, when I opened the box, my father's hand would shoot out and grab me. It would pull me into the dark box where I would suffocate because the darkness was so thick that I couldn't inhale it. When I woke, I was gasping and sweaty. I would pray, "Thank you, God, that it was only a dream. Please keep Pops in jail forever. Amen."

The vivid dream scared me so much that I was uncomfortable opening the mailbox. I devised a method to open it with a stick. I would peek in from a few feet away to see if the dreaded hand was there ready to spring out and grab me, or if it was safe to pick the mail up. The hand in the mailbox never reached for me ... until one fateful day when I carefully opened the box with my stick and peeked in. Seeing nothing, I reached in to pick up the lone piece of mail, and there it was ... addressed to me ... a letter from Pops!

A flood of suffocating guilt washed over me. I didn't want to know what might be written on the pages of that repugnant letter. Probably some reference to those shameful things I did ... was forced to do. *Don't single me out anymore! Leave me alone ... leave me alone!* I looked around quickly to see if anyone was watching. When I determined that the coast was clear, I folded the letter and stuck it in my shoe.

"Any mail?" Mom asked when I reached the house.

"Nope, nothing," I said, sprinting up the stairs to my tiny room. Once in my room, I took the letter from my shoe and hid it in a folded stocking in my dresser drawer; then I hurried down to help Chuck and Willie, who were cleaning the lunch dishes away. I didn't want to churn up any unwelcome interest in what I was doing.

The letter had to be burned unread; there was nothing else to do with it. I decided I would burn it as soon as I was alone. I didn't want to read anything written by Pops. I didn't want his words in my mind and possibly lodging there. I knew he would talk as though I was his confidant and a partner in his disgusting filth. It made me sick with shame.

Don't bother me again, you bastard! I thought, but unfortunately it was not the last letter to arrive, and I hid them unread as they came. The letters and the shame of having been exposed as a victim of incest in the local newspaper took a heavy toll on me. It was even more difficult to attend school now, since my secret was out, and the endless stares were ever present.

Maybe it was not my place, but I often looked at my mother and wondered if she was able to understand just how tenuous our situation really was. Could she foresee all the pitfalls that might befall our little group? She seemed oblivious to all of them, going about her day as though we were just a normal family.

I watched her stirring something on the stove. Her face was tranquil, expressionless, and I felt anxious, almost annoyed. She never really thought about anything, she just accepted whatever rolled over her. *Do you know you're pregnant? Do you know how difficult it is for Willie, Chuck, and me to attend school now that everyone knows about us? Are you aware that normal people don't care to befriend kids involved in incest and abuse ... that nothing can change the stares and whispers, not even Mr. Brody ... Do you know, Mom?*

This was my last year of school at the Tanner District School, and I couldn't wait to finish so I could go where no one knew who I was.

It was the tenth of April, and Mr. Brody was holding an Easter egg hunt during the noon hour. When the hour arrived, we couldn't wait to burst through the double doors and run helter-skelter around the schoolyard looking for eggs. We charged through the doors with our empty baskets. Char grabbed my hand and squeezed it, and I shook her hand away. I felt a sudden rush of something between annoyance and rage. I moved around the yard, unable to shake the feeling.

I don't want your damned pity, I thought. *It's easy to have fun and burgers and lots of friends if you're normal. If you're normal, you can run around looking for eggs, as if you have a life filled with everything good. Maybe if someone put your father's name in the newspaper and told something horrid about you, you'd understand. I hate you, Char! You're a smug jerk ... Die!*

Driving home after school in our pathetic wagon, I couldn't help but think of how much I hated my life, and to be honest I started to feel a little sorry for myself ... okay, face it, extremely sorry for myself! I wanted more. I wanted a life! I wanted to be normal too ... like Char. We bumped along in our little wagon, as we had so many times before. "I don't want to do this anymore," I said.

"What the hell are you talkin' about?" Willie said, shaking his head.

"I want something more, Willie. I'm going to get away from here," I said, searching Willie's face for a sign of approval.

He shook his head slowly back and forth in disbelief. "You're fuckin' nuts," he said flatly, taking my hand. "Don't get your hopes up, Franny; you'll just get hurt again."

I pulled my hand away. "Don't say that word, Willie," I said.

"Willie can say fuckin' if he wants to," Chuck chimed in, frowning at me. "He's the man, not you."

I rode the rest of the way home in silence, dreaming of a better life, a life where nobody knew my name and I was like Char ... normal.

The unwelcome letters kept coming. This was a big problem for me; I had to guard the mailbox to make sure that my secret wasn't disclosed to the rest of the family. It was more difficult on school days because the box was located so that we passed it on the way home. I didn't want my brothers to find out I was receiving letters from Pops.

I positioned myself so that I would be closest to the mailbox as we drove by in our wagon. That way, I would be the one who would be expected to pick the mail out of the box. We'd pull up to the mailbox and I would hop out. "I'll walk in," I'd call to my brothers.

"Okay," they'd answer over their shoulders without stopping. When they had gone a short distance, I'd stand back and open the box with my stick. On this particular day, there was a large manila envelope addressed to Mrs. Mary Beck. "Hmmm … What is this about?" I was surprised to see my mother's name printed out on the envelope instead of "Mrs. Nicholas Beck … hmmm … Mary Beck." *I like that,* I thought. "Mary Beck … Mary Beck."

When I came into the house, Mom was in the kitchen. "Mary Beck, a letter came for you!" I announced.

Mom looked surprised. "Oh it did, did it?" she teased, with her broad toothless smile.

I felt my heart swell a little. I saw a flicker of something in her. This was a glimpse into the life we could have had. *God,* I asked, *why?*

I flopped into a chair, tears wet on my cheeks. Mom saw me, and she came and knelt down before me. "Franny, your whole life is before you," she said. "It'll be all right."

I wiped my eyes, "I love you, Mary Beck, now open your mail, please!" I said, handing Mom her big manila envelope. We tore into it together. Inside we found the results of our interview with the county caseworker. There were all kinds of forms to fill out if we wanted to receive aid from the county and a transcript of the interview we had given the caseworker. There were also consent forms for Mom to sign so the transcripts could be used in court for Pops' trial. It all looked so complicated and otherworldly. Mom and I looked at each other bewildered.

"Now what in the world is all of this?" Mom asked. "I'll have to talk to that attorney the county gave me," she said. "I'll see if he can tell me what to do. I'll call him next time Ernie checks on us."

"Mary Beck, I think you would want to call the case-worker for this," I said.

"I don't care who I talk to, so long as they can tell me what I will have to do ... and it's Mom to you!" she answered, flashing me a huge tooth-missing smile.

I laughed then from my heart. I realized that I wasn't afraid to laugh now. It felt good.

"Mary Beck, Mary Beck," I chanted.

"I'll Mary Beck you," she threatened, smirking.

"No more Mrs. Nick, its Mary Beck to me!" I teased.

The four of us shared a wonderful peaceful evening. My mother was right, my whole life was ahead of me. *I am going to make the best of this life,* I thought. Our wonderful friend, Ernie, didn't show up to check on us that evening; maybe he needed a break, too. He had been on duty since the very beginning of our "flight to freedom." He probably wondered if he was stuck with us for life.

Chapter 15

We had barely finished breakfast the next morning when Ernie rapped quietly. "Am I here too early? I have a message for you."

"No, Ernie," I said. "Mary Beck will be with you shortly."

Ernie smiled and nodded. "Why thank you, Franny, that's very kind of you."

Mom came to the door where Ernie waited. "Telephone call for Mrs. Beck," he said.

"You may call me Mary Beck if you wish, Ernie," she said, throwing me a meaningful glance.

"My pleasure, Mary Beck," Ernie answered. "I shall."

"It's Mary to my friends, Ernie ... it's Mary to you! Now where is that big envelope we got yesterday?" Mom asked. I gave her the envelope, and she took it with her when she went to use Ernie's phone. He held the door and took her arm when she slid in.

I noticed that my mother's speech had changed since Pops was gone, and she had an opportunity to converse with Ernie. It had reverted back to the more refined verbal communication skills she was taught in her childhood. I thought that was rather remarkable, because it hadn't been that long since Pops was jailed. As always, I wanted my share of anything good, so I decided that I would improve my verbal skills as well.

Willie, Chuck, and I worked on daily chores while Mom was gone. My mother put me in charge of the operation; my two brothers resented my authority over them and showed their displeasure by polluting the atmosphere with expletives. Between profanities, they would spit to express their total disdain for me. It's amazing what lengths some people will go to in order to express their autonomy. My brothers were an endless source of amusing capers, and I enjoyed it more than they could have guessed.

I kept my silence and let them perform their little dance with the devil. By the time Ernie and Mom rolled into the driveway, I had heard every profane word that had ever been uttered since the beginning of human existence.

"I guess I'll have to admit to Mom that I lost control of you filthy-mouthed boys," I said. Before they could answer me, the car door opened and Mom stepped out. "Oh Mom," I said, "I will tell you how things went today a little later, after I finish my chores." Willie and Chuck shot each other "the look," and Mom looked at me knowingly.

Willie volunteered to help me with my chores so that he could try to make amends for the day before I had a chance to talk to Mom. Unfortunately for him, Ernie opened the trunk and hauled out two bags of groceries just then. Mom decided to join in the game. "Help Ernie with the groceries, Willie," she said, throwing me another meaningful glance. He took the two bags from Ernie and carried them into the house, looking back at me furtively. I was delirious with joy!

I loved my two brothers for their quirky little ways. I would never have squealed on them.

Mom talked to Ernie for a minute or two before he waved goodbye and left. While we ate dinner that evening, she told us that she would be going into Fargo to talk to her attorney and to rehearse for the trial. "I will have to be in the court-room with 'you know who' during the trial," she said. "Monday, I have to go into Fargo to practice answering questions that might be asked by his attorney. The questions are going to be as harsh as they can make them. They will be trying to confuse me so I look like I'm lying about him."

She looked across the table and caught Willie's eyes. "I've never been this nervous, and I've been scared all my life," she said, tearing up a little bit.

"Mom," he said, getting up and coming around the table. "Everything is going to be all right. You're doing the right thing." He put his hand on her shoulder and kissed her hair. "I love you, Mom," he said. "Just tell the truth."

"I'm getting to be such a crybaby," she answered, dropping her head to hide the tears. "Oh, and guess what? Your father is fit to stand trial. That was their finding."

Of course I never told on my two brothers for their day of cursing, profanity, and spitting. We had learned to stick together long ago. My brothers were my heart, especially Willie. There were many times, when the world seemed to be against me, that Willie would hold me, or he would get me a glass of water after I had been attacked and stroke my hair. We had survived many hard times because we had each other, although my conscience wasn't completely clear on this subject either.

I heard Mom during the night fixing something to eat or drink, and I knew she was having a rough night. I was reminded again of how much she feared Pops, and I remembered the physical and mental abuse we had all suffered. I dropped over the edge of my bed onto my knees and thanked God that we were safe from Pops.

None of the children in our family was allowed to testify because the courts were afraid we would be traumatized. *That's a joke,* I thought. *If we were to testify before the jury, we would probably traumatize them.*

Monday rolled around, and Ernie showed up like he always did. *God bless you, Ernie!* Mom was ready to go and slipped into the car before we even had time to give her an "Atta girl."

The day dragged on unending. It seemed to last forever. I wondered what kind of preparation Mom was going through. No one knew better than I what Mom's limitations were. I knew she would probably clam up if the going got too tough. I hoped she would be open to the instructions she was given and not shut that quirky mind of hers and retreat into the safety of her eccentricities. *Stay with us, Mom,* I thought.

I saw the mailman stop at our box, so I went to gather the mail. I was still opening the mailbox with a stick, and I scolded myself, "Coward! What's wrong with you?" I opened it with a stick anyway just to be on the safe side. Inside I found a letter from my grandmother. I ripped it open anxiously, hungry for her precious words.

To my great sorrow, my grandfather had died peacefully while sleeping in his favorite easy chair. A gentle heart simply quit beating at a predestined time. Grandma Nina had tried to wake him and found that he was dead. He had died as he lived, with dignity and grace. I never felt more like making my life a reflection of his than when I read the lines of her letter. I thought, *if I'm good, maybe my end can be as poetic as my grandfather's.* "God, I want to be good," I said aloud. I was surprised how little and impotent my voice sounded.

The letter, written in my grandmother's shaky hand, asking my mother if she could take the time to visit her and attend Grandpa's funeral read in part:

… and so it breaks my heart to tell you that your Father left us quietly as he slept Tuesday afternoon, and the world is the lesser for it. I do hope that you will be able to attend his service.

I have read some of the horrifying stories about Nick in the paper. My heart breaks for you and my grandchildren, and I know that you have your hands full with the trial. If you can make time to come and bid your father goodbye that would be wonderful. If you cannot he will understand.

I know that your life has been a misery to you, my dearest Mary, and I want to help you in any way I can. You know there will always be a home for you and my grandchildren here with me.

Your father and I had planned to come to you until his passing. Now I rely on you, to make your way here, to see me as soon as you can. If this is not possible, I will ask your brother to bring me to you.

I love you, Mother

I folded the letter and put it into the envelope again. I regretted not having waited for Mom to come home so she could have opened it for herself, even though it was customary for anyone who gathered the mail to open Grandma's letters. With the exception of Pops, of course; letters from my grandparents never came when Pops gathered the mail … Curious, isn't it?

Willie and Chuck read Grandma's letter, and the three of us sat in silence anticipating Mom's reaction to this news. Willie comforted me, wiping my tears away with his fingers. He told me that everything would be all right. We were afraid that this was the straw that would break the camel's back. We vacillated between excitement for Grandma's visit and grief for the loss of Grandpa Mat. We spent our afternoon this way.

The shadows were lengthening now, and we were forced out of a sense of duty to take care of our evening chores and make something for dinner. Once the chores were completed, we tackled the culinary end of things. None of us knew how to cook, but we made a valiant effort. It was a disaster! We ate what we could and tidied the kitchen up.

Mom still wasn't home. We weren't accustomed to her being gone, and we were feeling anxious. Finally we saw headlights flashing here and there, as Ernie's car made the curves in the dirt road leading to our house.

Chapter 16

Mom flopped into a chair. "I'm beat!" she groaned, "I don't know if I can remember everything they told me. Have you eaten anything?" she asked, looking around the kitchen.

"Yup, we have. Are you hungry, Mom?" I asked

"No, Ernie bought me dinner after my question-and-answer session," she said.

Thank God, I thought. *You'd play hell getting anything fit to eat here.*

"Oh, and did I tell you Pops is sane enough to be tried?" she asked. "I guess they aren't very fussy. Ha!"

"You told us before, Mom," Willie said.

"What's that, a letter from Mother? Give it here, I need a boost, and you kids go to bed *now*, it's late."

"Mom," I said, "the letter … it's bad … it's Grandpa!"

She didn't answer me. She took the letter carefully out of the envelope and slowly read it. When she had finished, she pressed the letter to her breast and closed her eyes. She was struggling to accept the news without bitterness. "We were lucky to have had him," she said. "Go to bed now, all of you," she ordered, still clutching the letter to her heart. "I can't talk; I have to be alone right now."

My brothers and I reluctantly started to leave. "We'll talk in the morning," she called after us.

I'll never know how long Mom stayed up that night, because I slept almost immediately, and in the morning I felt guilty that I hadn't mourned with her. I woke to the smell of breakfast, and I hurried down the rickety stairs to be with her and to see if she was all right after getting the news about her father's death. Another reason was that I wanted to hear all about her ordeal with the attorney. I wanted to encourage her to keep a cool head when she was on the stand.

"So Mom," I said, "how was your question-and-answer session yesterday?"

"Oh my God!" she answered. "You can't imagine! It was tough."

I could see that her face was flushed a little, and she was agitated. I couldn't understand why Grandpa had to pick this time, of all times, to leave her. She always had a deep love for her parents and often told wonderful stories about the times they had together. His death added the burden of loss and loneliness to the confusion she already felt ... Life goes on.

This would be the first time she saw Nick since the night he was arrested. I was concerned that once she saw him, she would be frightened of him, and say whatever she thought would please him; after all, she was accustomed to pleasing him ... if she could. I had to find a way to tell her that there was no turning back now.

"You know, Mom, it's really important for you to remember everything they told you when you were in Fargo."

She nodded without looking at me, and I knew that she wasn't sure she could remember everything. I wanted to tell her again and again until I forced her to understand, with perfect clarity, that she must not try to please Pops. He must not win this time.

I had absolutely no confidence in her. Even weighing the conviction she had when we made our way across the river against her sometimes easy, careless nature didn't inspire confidence, but it was reassuring to think again of her bravery that night. The problem was, once she felt those cunning black eyes of his attached to her in stony hatred, would she revert back to trying to please him? Would she blubber about him being a good father or tell the jury that he really wasn't a bad man?

Mom was a wonderful person. She could be funny and even clever at times, but she just wasn't capable of fending off sophisticated innuendo and avoiding the verbal traps that might be sprung on her in a trial. I was feeling a little desperate. I remembered times when she came to me asking what was meant by something someone had said to her in conversation, and I hoped she would understand all the questions asked of her before she gave her answer. Maybe she would surprise everyone.

"Mom, will you be having another session with your attorney before the trial?"

"Oh, yes, we are going to meet again today. They'll call Ernie when they're ready."

"When is the trial, Mom?"

"It's going to be held this coming Tuesday," she answered.

"You mean next week Tuesday?" I asked.

"Yes, that's right," she said, "next week Tuesday."

"Oh crap! That's really close!" I said.

"Yes, it is, Franny. He sent a bunch of questions for me to study. You read them to me, and I'll try to answer them while we eat. I'm really hungry. I'm eating for two!"

"Okay. Where are they?" I said.

Things were reaching a fever pitch now. It seemed as though we had been standing still waiting for a resolution to our problem with Pops, never knowing what was going to transpire or when. The uncertainty that plagued us inspired nightmares that Pops would get away somehow and come home to finish what he had started. Now the trial was upon us. My mother was a nervous wreck, making her plans for the day of the trial and rehearsing her story.

Willie and I nagged incessantly to go to the trial with her. She wouldn't hear of it, because she had been advised by her attorney that we were not to attend. County caseworker Lucille Adams picked this time to make a visit and sealed our fate. We were not going to the trial, a fact that was becoming quite clear. My mother, brothers, and I could never have imagined how our absence from the trial would affect the outcome of its verdict.

When Nick was led into the courtroom, he smiled at Mary and waved his hand, as you would to an old friend. She didn't respond to his overture but cast her eyes down to avoid his.

He looked around as though he was trying to locate someone in the room. He continued to watch the door until it was time to take the oath.

"Where's the kids?" He mouthed the words to Mary; she ignored him.

The judge banged his gavel, announcing that the court was in session, and routinely asked, "Will the defendant please rise and state your name for the court?"

Nick answered him by saying he would rather not say anything until his kids were in the courtroom.

"The court is in session, sir, please rise and state your name for the court!" the judge repeated.

Holding his hand up dismissively, Nick articulated each word slowly and quietly. "Git … my … kids … in … here!" he said.

"You will please rise and state your name for the court," the judge insisted.

"When my kids'r here maybe I will," he declared.

"The defendant will rise and state his name for the court!" the judge demanded. "The court is in session! Counsel will advise his client to rise and state his name for the court."

"Nick, stand up and tell them your name for God's sake!" his attorney ordered.

Nick slammed his huge fist down on the table so hard the table bounced, spilling water and scattering the neatly stacked papers his attorney had placed there.

"You are in contempt, sir!" the judge admonished, banging his gavel.

"Contempt my ass, I ain't gonna say a Goddamn thing till them kids is here!" Nick bellowed. Rearing up and sending his chair clattering to the floor, he turned his attention to his attorney. "I told ya ta have them damn kids in here! I ain't sayin nothing till ya git-em in here!"

"Please sit down, Nick."

"You shut yer fuckin' mouth or yer gonna find out why ya never wan-na lie ta me!"

"You are in contempt, sir!" The judge raised his voice, his gavel banging, and his face turning red. "You are in con-tempt!"

"Nick, I'm trying to help you … Please calm down and be quiet," his attorney said.

"I'm gun-na show them little bastards what they done to me, what they caused ta happen," Nick boomed.

"Nick, for the love of God … *please shut up!*"

"Shut-up?" he asked, as he turned his massive body to-ward his attorney in a stare-down. Then, unable to contain himself any longer, he grabbed the man and flung him to-ward the judge like a rag doll. "Shut-up yerself!" he yelled.

Then he turned his attention to Mary. Throwing chairs this way and that, he plowed a path to reach her before the court guards could stop him. Grabbing her hair he swung her out of the chair, and she fell to the floor in terror. "Ya know I'm gonna kill ya now, don't cha, ya dirty bitch!" he bellowed.

Her attorney held his hand up. "Stay away, Mr. Beck," he warned impotently.

The courtroom was in chaos. Several uniformed police swarmed Nick and subdued him, but not before he managed to land a blow to Mary's back, sending her sprawling on her elbows across the floor of the courtroom as she struggled to fend off his attack.

His rage, strength, and size were almost too much for the police to handle, but in the end he was cuffed and dragged away. When he returned, he was muzzled and bound. No more ranting and throwing things.

His attorney made a plea on his behalf. "My client wants to plead 'not guilty,' your honor," he said sheepishly to the judge.

Nick was not a happy suspect when Mary told her story, especially about the molestation. He struggled to throw off his restraints when she pointed out his trusty old cattle whip and described how she had acquired scars that were shown in the photos of her back and arms. His body writhed as he used his immense strength against his constraints. When he failed to break free, he tried to kill her with his eyes, so filled with hatred that they appeared to be those of Satan.

Surprisingly calm, Mary met his stare with a look of great sadness and quietly answered the questions. In an ironic twist, her testimony had been confirmed by Nick's own words and actions at the beginning of the trial. Indeed, Nick Beck had already confirmed that he was guilty.

It took the jury less than an hour to find him guilty of assault with intent to do bodily harm, assault with a deadly weapon, child abuse, child molestation, spousal abuse, reckless endangerment, and attempted homicide.

Nick was sentenced to five years in prison for each count to be served consecutively, and one additional year for contempt of court.

Thirty-six years in prison.

When he heard the sentence, he closed his eyes and dropped his head. He was finally subdued. He hadn't expected this. He thought he would be in jail overnight or spend a few weeks in jail, tops, and it would be home again to punish his antagonists. He could tell his neighbors that he was accused falsely.

He was wrong! The judge in Fargo, North Dakota, didn't look fondly on this sort of activity. My father was awarded the maximum time the judge could muster.

Mary had full custody of the boys and me now. That was the heaviest punishment of all. Nick's attorney asked her if they could visit Nick in prison, but she told him she would have to think about it. "I'm tired, I can't think of anything right now," she said. "I'll let you know."

Ernie helped her with her jacket. "Do you think you could stand a good cup of coffee and a bite to eat, Mary?"

"You read my mind, Ernie," she said. He took her arm and they left the courtroom.

A huge burden had fallen from her shoulders. Nick could no longer control her … couldn't hurt her or her kids … he had lost control of them. It was a day she would never forget.

She felt an undeniable sadness mixed with all of that relief she was feeling. Nick went to jail, and she got out of prison on the same day. Justice had been served. She wondered why she felt such sorrow for Nick. He was surely a monster, but why?

Chapter 17

Willie, Chuck, and I waited for Mom to come home from the trial. We were anxious to hear what had transpired in the courtroom, what the verdict had been, and whether Pops was coming home or not. When we heard the car turn into our driveway, we ran to the window, filled with excitement and fear, but we didn't recognize the car.

Lucille Adams had left some time ago. Our first thought was that she was returning for something she had forgotten, but we soon found to our great glee that it was Grandma Nina and Uncle Paul. We were frenzied when we recognized them. I ran around trying to tidy up the kitchen because Grandma's house was always neat, and I didn't want her to be disappointed with ours. My brothers scampered out to greet them.

I soon gave up my project and ran to meet them with my brothers. Grandma always smelled so nice. I loved that smell and inhaled deeply when she hugged me to her breast. "Grandma, Grandma, I'm so glad you came," I said.

"I love you, child," she answered. "I love you with all my heart."

"Grandma, Mom is gone. She is in court today," I said.

"Oh my! In court, you say?"

"Yes, in court about Pops," I said.

"Oh my!" she said.

"Grandma, there are a lot of things that happened. Please don't ask me to tell you about anything. Mom will tell you."

"I will never ask you to tell me anything, dear. If you want me to know something, you will have to ask me to listen," she assured me.

"I'm sorry that Grandpa is gone. I wish I could have seen him before he died," I told her. "I feel bad for you, Grandma."

"Oh, but you did see him before he died, dear, many times, and he loves you … Still, I do miss him too. We were very happy together. Our only real sadness was when … well, someday I will tell you all about it, dear, but for now we'll enjoy being together. That's enough for me."

Uncle Paul volunteered to help Willie and Chuck with the outside chores so that I could stay inside with Grandma Nina. I thought I should make dinner, but I had never cooked anything and had no idea what to do.

"I don't know what to fix, Grandma. I want to make something good for dinner, but I don't know what to fix."

"I have a marvelous idea, Franny," she said. "Let's make pancakes. Pancakes are my meal of choice when I'm desperate for a quick meal. How does that sound? I hope you have bacon! I like bacon with them," she said.

"Yup, we do," I told her.

"Do you mean 'yes, we do'?" she asked.

"I do mean 'yes, we do,'" I told her.

When Mom and Ernie got home, we were just finishing our pancakes with bacon and eggs. Grandma Nina could make anything taste good.

Mom brought Ernie in with her and introduced him to Grandma Nina and Uncle Paul. Together they recounted the ordeal Mom had gone through. They talked late into the night. Many of the pressing issues now facing Mom were discussed by the four adults, along with possible solutions. We children listened with great interest to all of the talking and laughter.

Finally, Ernie rose from the table. "I have had more excitement than any one man can stand in one day. I think I will mosey along. It has been a great pleasure to meet you both; perhaps we will have the good fortune of visiting again soon."

"The pleasure is mine, Ernie," Paul said, extending his hand. The four of them walked to Ernie's car together. My brother and I stayed in the doorway watching as they shook hands and exchanged pleasantries.

"I feel real bad for Pops," Willie said. "Was he always mean?"

"Willie, a long time ago Mom says he was nice once in a great while, but that's a long time ago. He isn't nice, and he's not going to change."

"Are they going to stay over or drive home, Franny?" Willie asked, motioning toward the car with his head.

"They won't stay. It's not that far, they'll go home tonight," I told him. "They would be uncomfortable staying here anyway."

"Should I stay up 'til they go, or do you think it would be all right for me to go to bed now?"

"Go ahead, Willie, Chuck is already sleeping," I said.

Ernie drove away, and they all came in and started to pick up and prepare to leave.

"It's past my bedtime," Paul said. "Let's hit the road."

After Grandma and Uncle Paul left, Mom asked me how I would feel about moving in with Grandma at the ranch.

"Really?" I asked.

"We'll sleep on it," she answered.

Part Three

Chapter 18

Sometimes wonderful things just happen out of necessity, and so it was decided that we were going to move into Grandmother Lawrence's house, at least until we were squared away. Uncle Paul made sure that someone was hired to work the fields at our old farm, to plant and harvest them. He supervised the work and conducted transactions with the local elevators when the crop was sold and found buyers for the livestock, even Pops' horse.

Willie spent every waking hour at Uncle Paul's side. Paul, like Grandfather, was soft-spoken and thoughtful. Willie admired him and tried to impress him with swagger and tough talk, but he soon learned that Uncle Paul was not impressed by profanity.

"Please spare me, Willie. I dislike profanity, and I prefer that you keep a lid on it while we're together."

"What did I say?" Willie asked.

"Think before you speak, Willie. Think! What did you say that I would object to?"

"I didn't say nothin'."

"You didn't say *anything*, Willie. Respect yourself, and respect those around you. Get it?"

"You're worse than Franny," Willie mumbled, rolling his eyes. Paul couldn't suppress a tiny smile but didn't answer him.

Willie found a hero in Paul, one he needed so badly. He would have preferred that the hero in his life was his biological father, but that could never be. He had tried to be loyal to Pops, even after the man almost beat him to death, but Willie finally admitted to himself that Pops wasn't even a friend. Now he had the opportunity to see how a real man conducted himself, and he liked it. It was painful to watch Willie struggle between what he had known for most of his life and his new reality. He emulated Uncle Paul's strong intellectual approach to life.

Then there was Chuck, who in the past had defended Willie's right to say "fuck" whenever he wanted to, only to find now that Willie no longer needed a lingo defender.

"You think you're smart, don't you, *big* Willie," Chuck accused.

"What are you talking about, Chuck?"

"I'm talking about a guy with a brown ring around his big, fat nose, that's what."

"Think before you speak," Willie crooned smugly.

"You're not my friend, you fucker!" Chuck retorted, glancing here and there to see if he had been overheard.

"Have some respect for yourself, Chuck, and for those around you. Get it!" Willie smiled inwardly, feeling full of himself.

"Girl baby!" Chuck screeched. "You're nuttin' but a little girl punk!"

Paul heard the exchange, unseen by the boys. He realized he had made a mistake by not including Chuck in the things he did with Willie. Paul let Chuck know that he was as important as his bigger brother by making sure he was invited to participate in those things and to work hand in hand with the two of them. *That will cure a foul mouth quicker than a reprimand at this point,* Paul reasoned. *He's just a little boy, and he has been through too much already.*

Mom and I loved the beautiful old house with its dark-wood floors and furniture pieces that looked as though there were dozens of coats of wax on them. I soon found out that Grandma Nina was obsessed with cleanliness. She never let her guard down. When we first moved there, it was really quite painful learning and following all the rules. I will always have that memory of her.

"Who used this?" she would ask, holding a cup or a sock or a kitchen utensil or something else up for us to see. "If you take it out, put it back. If you use it, wash it. If you get it dirty, clean it," she would say. "That's how we do it. Am I right?" One of us would have to come forward, claim whatever it was, and put it back where we found it. Grandma never raised her voice, but none of us dared defy her for some unknown reason.

I secreted the packet of letters I had received from Pops into my things when we moved to Grandma's ranch. Now I was looking for a place to discard them. I thought of several options. I could burn them. I could bury them. I could tear them into a million pieces and let the wind blow them away. I could hide them somewhere and hope they would never be found.

I had no idea that Uncle Paul had intercepted several of them that were delivered after we moved away and had destroyed them. He had also asked Ernie to check now and then and to pick up any letters that were delivered so that they would not be used to further the rumors that flourished about us ... about me.

I wanted a whole new life. Things were so different here. So beautiful and tranquil, and no one knew who I was. I liked that. I liked it a lot. I guess that must have been what inspired me to feel such urgency about disposing of those unwelcome letters. I wanted to eradicate everything that had gone before, to stamp it out of existence.

I would stand in front of the mirror and deny that it was I who suffered the molestation. *Hello, my name is Frances. Did you call me Franny? Please! I don't respond to Franny. I prefer Frances. That's right, Frances ... Frances Lawrence, that's my name. Oh yeah, that girl. I heard about what happened to her, but I never really knew her. How awful. Can you imagine?*

That's when I decided that I would burn the letters, and the sooner the better. I stuck the letters in my sleeve and found Grandma Nina in the kitchen.

"Grandma Nina, may I start a fire outside in the fire pit?" I asked.

"Why do you want to fire up that old thing, dear?"

"I want to make s'mores," I lied.

"I'll gather the ingredients, Franny, and you make the fire. How does that sound?"

"Grandma, please call me Frances," I said. "If I could have only one wish, it would be that everyone would call me Frances and not Franny. Will you? Please?"

"My goodness! That's a wonderful idea. Frances and not Franny, I certainly will."

I started the fire using the letters as kindling. The flames grew tall, and all those unread words symbolizing my lousy childhood rose in an impotent wisp of smoke and were swallowed up by the universe. It was a good feeling! *Oh yeah! I heard what happened to that girl Franny, but I never really knew her. Did you?*

That night when we were eating dinner, Grandma Nina told my brothers and my mom that I had asked to be called Frances. Willie and Chuck looked at me contemptuously and snickered. Grandma held them in her gaze, saying, "It probably doesn't seem important to some of us, but Frances is her name, and she prefers to be called by her proper name. For my part, I think that would be entirely appropriate, and I'm sure everyone agrees with me. Am I right?"

The next step in my plan was to have my last name changed to Lawrence. There was only one way that I could think of to achieve my objective. *Now*, I thought, *I must convince Mom to divorce Pops somehow and to take her maiden name back and to give my brothers and me new names as well. After all, it would be very confusing if we had names other than the one belonging to our very own mother.*

I immediately thought of Grandma Nina. If I could convince her, it would be a done deal. I began to formulate a plan to convince Grandma to suggest the divorce. I had to be careful not to let Mom know I had anything to do with it until after Grandma approached her. She might resist, and I wanted the name changed before my first day in my new high school. I felt pressed for time. *After my plan has taken effect,* I thought, *I will be free of that poor pitiful incest victim's image.*

I could see myself signing my name "Frances Faye Lawrence." Then it came to me: I would use my middle name first and my first name in the middle. *Faye Frances Lawrence ... Faye Lawrence, how divine!*

Hello, my name is Faye Lawrence ... No, I don't believe I've ever heard anything about a girl named Franny until this very moment. How awful for her. Too bad! Did she survive? ... Not really!

Chapter 19

"Willie, I think you sort of look like Uncle Paul. Have you ever noticed that?" I said, trying to set the hook. "I swear you could be father and son."

"I never gave it any thought one way or another," he answered. I noticed that he didn't hate the thought.

"It would be wonderful to have a dad as nice and kind as Uncle Paul, wouldn't it, Willie?" I probed.

"Oh man, he's a great guy," Willie said.

"I know," I answered. "My brother Willie Lawrence, that sounds so fine," I flung over my shoulder as I left, not wanting to push too hard. I wanted him to think it was he who wanted to be a Lawrence. I left Willie to his thoughts and ran to the house.

I heard my mom and grandma talking, and I stopped outside the screen door to listen to them for a moment. It was apparent that Grandma had asked Mom about the changes that were taking place in her body.

"Oh my, Mary, I had no idea that you and he were together in that way. I'm not sure I approve of that sort of thing."

. "You don't have a choice, mother. He takes what he wants. You know that!" Mary's voice rose.

"Good grief, Mary, no, I didn't know that. I am certainly disappointed in both of you ... and you, Mary, you're married to someone else," Nina reprimanded. "It's disgraceful, dear; I had no idea Mr. Cranston was the sort of man who would force himself on you."

"Ernie has nothing to do with this, Mother. It was Nick!" Mary retorted.

"That monster? Goodness, Mary! I'll help you through this as much as I can."

"Help with what, Grandma?" I asked, stepping in from my post outside the door. I took pleasure in having prior knowledge of their conversation, and I felt a little powerful. I knew more than they thought I did.

"Nothing that concerns you, dear, it's a talk between your mother and I," she said, defusing me.

"Girl talk?" I teased.

"You will know when we decide to tell you," she answered sternly.

One by one, the pieces to the puzzle were coming together. The fact that Grandma was going to help Mom with her pregnancy removed a huge worry from my mind. Now I could concentrate on acquiring the name I so desired. I had a little over two months left before my first day in my new school. Two months to execute my plans for a new name and a new life. My new life! I felt my heart surge. Oh yes, this was going to happen ... *No one can stop me now,* I thought ... *No one!*

There was never a method devised that could calculate the amount of importance I placed on escaping the stigma of my past. I detested the sympathetic looks and words from well-meaning people blabbing away as though I was defined by the disgusting experiences that had been forced on me. I would smile and think, *Shut your rotten mouths; I am not that girl. Do you understand that? You bastards.*

It seemed that since I had escaped my abuser, I was angry much of the time. I don't know if it was anger or if I was suffering from a severe case of extreme impatience, but it was definitely triggered many times each day. Fortunately, I possessed the art of deception. My calm demeanor and my generous smile were a veneer on the surface hiding a tempest inside.

I began to live within my obsession. *Hello, my name is Faye. That's right … Faye Lawrence. What? You say there has been an incestuous assault on a girl named Franny Beck? I don't want to seem cold, but why would that concern me? I never knew her.*

My mind was filled with plans about my new school. My new life! I wanted so many things. One of the things I wanted was a new hairstyle. I searched through magazines and saw wonderful hairstyles that I thought Faye would look good in. I worried that I would not have a wardrobe that would suit Faye. She mustn't look like a ragamuffin, and certainly nothing like Franny with her old-fashioned hand-me-downs. I wanted clothes, and I wanted clothes with style that would fit me. Nothing was too good for Faye Lawrence.

The more I considered the daunting venture that I was embarking on, the more I thought that I would probably get more help from my Uncle Paul than anyone else in the family. My mom and grandma were not very fashion-forward. Talking fashion with them would be like teaching someone a foreign language that you hadn't learned yet. They were very conservative, and I wasn't much better. I determined to ask my uncle if he would take me shopping and to a stylist before school started. I would hope that my brothers and I would all go shopping. I didn't want them to look like backwoodsmen, because that had the potential of blowing my cover.

"Uncle Paul, I just don't know what I'm going to do. I'm desperate. I have nothing to wear to the new school, and I'm afraid Mom will try to make my clothes again. I'll be stuck wearing those ugly rags again ... Everyone will laugh at me. I don't even want to go if I have to go through that again. Please! Please! Help me, Uncle Paul." I hadn't realized how much anxiety was pent up in my mind about this, but as I was talking, tears began to flow. Once the well was primed, I couldn't stop. I, who never cried or at least cried very seldom, couldn't stop crying.

"Please don't cry, Franny ... Francis ... Faye, whatever! Let me think about it," he said.

Embarrassed, I ran up the stairs to take refuge from his obvious astonishment at my fit of crying. Unfortunately, Uncle Paul hadn't given me his answer before I sprinted away. Once in my room, I regained my composure. I looked in the mirror at my puffy red face, and I felt disgusted.

Is this the best you can do? I asked myself. *Now he has time to think, and he will probably act out of logic instead of sympathy ... Is that what you want, stupid girl? You should have gotten a commitment from him when you had the opportunity. Now it's probably too late! Oh, you should get used to wearing homemade rags, because you'll probably be wearing them for a long time!*

I looked back into the mirror, but Faye was not there; it was just Franny looking back with her puffy little face. She was small and lonely-looking. I had no sympathy for her. I hated her! I crawled into bed with my clothes on and pulled the covers over my head. I refused dinner that evening, saying that I was not feeling well.

Uncle Paul was the captain that kept everything running smoothly at the huge Lawrence estate. He had been groomed for years to do exactly that, and he ran a very tight ship.

Early the morning after my "sleep-in," Paul called a family meeting to "talk about how the family should handle schooling for the children," as he put it. We would have breakfast first and then, before the day's duties, we would discuss school topics among other things. My heart exploded in my chest. This was the definitive answer to my request. I had no clue how it would go. I think I was more afraid of this than I had ever been of Pops' whip. Well, maybe not ... but I knew how that would end. This was a mystery.

Breakfast was almost impossible to eat. I swallowed chunks of food without tasting them. I whipped around the kitchen clearing the dishes away and wiping the table down. I poured coffee for the adults and finally took my place at the table to wait for Uncle Paul to quit reading his paper and start talking.

I really thought Uncle Paul might have a sadistic streak, since he slowly browsed through the paper before saying anything. He finally finished his coffee and folded his paper.

"We have a lot to talk about," he said. "I just have to tell you how happy I am that we're all together now. After my father left us, it was awfully lonely here. Now the house is full of family and filled with joy ... and occasional tears," he chuckled, looking at me. "I like that!

"Mary, you and the children have suffered enough. I'm sorry that your life hasn't been happy. I want to help you change all that if you let me … we want to help you change it," he said, glancing at Patty and Grandma Nina. "We think it would be best for all of us if you were to come home for good. We're family; we want you here with us … Of course, with the joy of family, there comes a new set of challenges," Uncle Paul continued. "I realize that."

"I've waited a long time for you and my grandchildren to come home, dear," Grandma Lawrence interjected, looking at Mary.

"You'll have to go to a new school, that's one thing we'll have to deal with," Paul continued. "Willie and Chuck will go to Highland Elementary, of course, and Fra … I mean, Faye will go to Camden High School. I'm sorry you won't be going together, but Faye, you'll have to go it alone this year. It'll be all right once you get used to it!" he assured me.

"Oh, that's too bad," I faked regret, my heart tripping with joy.

We talked about what the future would hold for us. It was my heart's desire unfolding before my eyes as though I had written the script myself. I remembered when Ernie had bought me a hamburger on the way home from Fargo the day we went to visit Willie in the hospital and I had imagined being normal, with hamburgers whenever I wanted them. Now I had everything. Hamburgers! It sounds silly, but when I had nothing it was very important to me.

Now I was promised an appointment with a hairdresser and a new wardrobe. All I wanted to do at that moment was to live here in peace and comfort and to forget all about

Franny … That left one more hurdle I must overcome—to acquire the name that would complete the package.

I had to get to Mom somehow. I had to convince her to take her maiden name back, and time was flying. Soon I would be registering in my new school. Finally, out of desperation, I decided that Grandma couldn't help me with this, Willie couldn't help me with it, and I must go to Mom directly and convince her that she should divorce Pops and change her name and that of her children to Lawrence.

I asked her if she remembered how we went across the mighty Mouse River and made our way to Fargo to escape Pops' abuse. I told her that we had not yet escaped completely because we had to live day by day with the shame associated with his name and that we would never be completely free until we shed that name and the stigma that went with it. I told her that she was beautiful now that her teeth were fixed and everything, but she was still dragging that ugly name around with her. "You have to fix that too, Mom, you have to get rid of him for good," I said.

Surprisingly, Mom agreed with me and said she would talk to Uncle Paul about it. Later that day, she told me that Paul had called his attorney and made an appointment for the following week. When the time finally came, we all loaded into Uncle Paul's car for the trip into Fargo. We met with his attorney, who prepared the paperwork to begin divorce proceedings and completed the paperwork to change Mom's name and that of her children back to Lawrence. We shopped after we had visited the attorney and stopped for dinner before we drove home. Home at last!

Just like that, my life was changed forever. It was a day to remember. The day I truly became Faye Lawrence ... that's my name. There was no sleep for me that night.

I rehearsed my name over and over. I rehearsed how I would talk and how I would walk. I thought about how I would wear my hair. What clothes I would wear. I tried my new clothes on and talked to myself in the mirror ... *Mirror, mirror on the wall, who's the fairest of them all?*

When I registered at Camden High School, I printed the name "Faye F. Lawrence" in the appropriate box and signed my name "Faye F. Lawrence" with pride. I spent four years at Camden High School. Uncle Paul and Grandma Nina provided everything I could possibly want, and I had an insatiable appetite for nice things.

I made casual friendships with several people during those four years, but none of them were really what I would call close friends. I didn't feel as though they knew me, and for my part, I preferred it that way. I was always mildly uncomfortable when anyone attempted to draw too near to me. To be honest, I didn't even miss my friend Char.

During my first year at Camden High School, my sister, Sharon, was born into a life of warmth and comfort. She was adored by my mother. The same face that had turned away from me without expression in my time of need was now aglow with love. There was no forgiving Sharon for this and for all the advantages that were showered on her. *What about me? This should have been my life.* Eaten by envy, I could barely stand to look at her. *That's all right,* I told myself; *I really don't need anyone except Faye ... that's right, Faye Lawrence ... the center of the universe.*

In my second year of high school, I became editor of the school newspaper and, in my senior year, I was voted Homecoming Queen. Imagine that! Faye Lawrence, Homecoming Queen! I have to admit, it was a small school, and there wasn't that much competition … still, for me it was a proud moment.

Some of my classmates commented that things came easy for me, as though I possessed some genetic intellectual advantage. In truth, I was probably just about average in intellect, but I had cleverness and a great need to rise above my inherited predisposition for mental differentness. I spent countless hours working on my studies—so much so that my grandma was driven to scold me from time to time and warn me that "all work and no play make Johnny a dull boy." Grandma Nina was always full of maxims.

Success wrought more success. It became easier to pull down good grades as time went by, but I was never satisfied and pressed constantly for better grades and more recognition. I had an endless need for approval.

Realizing early on that you were judged by how you spoke, I began to improve my speech, constantly adding words to my vocabulary and practicing to deliver them in a pleasing way. Grandma Nina told me on many occasions that it wasn't so much what you said, but how you said it, that makes the difference, so I began to imitate her and Uncle Paul. I loved their refined way of speaking. The Lawrence family migrated from England when Paul was a teenager, and my mother was a small child, they spoke with a British accent. I mimicked their vocabulary and speech pattern, as well as their soft British accents.

I was becoming a chameleon, changing myself whenever I chose and hiding the anger that constantly burned within me behind a warm, generous smile. I would stand before the mirror and rehearse ... *Yes, my name is Faye ... That's right, Faye Lawrence. Yes, thank you, that was me. I was Homecoming Queen, an honor I can assure you!*

I graduated from Camden High with honors and, as though I was living my own dream, Uncle Paul and Grandma Nina offered to subsidize my college. College! Uncle Paul told me that it would be a terrible waste if I didn't continue my education. I will never forget the feeling that swept over me when I got that high praise from someone I admired so much. "Thank you, Uncle Paul, I will do the best I can," I whispered. Tears welled up, and I turned away unable to speak. Intimacy was impossible for me. I could cope with many things, but not this.

Life in the dorm was nothing like the one I expected. I had imagined finding friends who I would value forever, but it never happened. My roommates were messy and loud. They had a wonderful zest for life, but I had no desire to emulate them. I shared my space with these strangers; my challenge was to preserve the relationship just as it was. I had no interest in cultivating friendships. More than anything, I missed my grandma and those wonderful hot breakfasts she served.

Laundry was relentless and, unlike my studies, it was out of control. It held the lowest position on my list of priorities. My grandma had spoiled me. When I told her about the problem I was having with my laundry, she invited me to bring it home.

"You have enough to do, love. You bring your laundry home and I will give it a proper washing."

"Are you sure, Grandma?" I asked.

"Do I look confused, dear?" she quizzed, then added, "It would please me immensely. Am I right?"

Once rid of my laundry dilemma, I was free to pursue my mission in life. I had finally put a face on it: it was that of Lucille Adams. Cool and polished, a child advocate with an expensive briefcase and shiny black pumps. I could close my eyes and see her face as though it was yesterday, but I wanted more … I wanted revenge.

I pictured myself being a prosecuting attorney, working to make sure that the truth was ripped from the throat of any child-molesting bastard who ever came up against me in a court of law!

My decision wasn't completely selfish. I really did want to help abused children overcome the stigma of abuse and the social rejection that comes with it. Already an expert on the subject of child abuse, I would be a natural, and it might be a wonderful way to collect some of the debt owed me for the years of abuse I had endured.

No one could have known how important it was to my battered siblings and me that we had family members who willingly gathered us into their protective embrace when we were finally rescued from our ordeal. Not all children are so lucky; many times, rescued families live in poverty and disgrace after an intervention. Who better than I to understand the plight of abused children? Who needed revenge more than I?

Once I had chosen my path, I immersed myself in my studies. Time flew by, one year piling on another. I lost myself in this world of academia—a world I came to view as insulated from real life, one composed only of narrowly defined thought, programmed response, and one's own feeling of superiority, the final goal in many cases. A place where the brain sought to dominate the heart and where intellectual arrogance was embraced as though it was some special prize to be coveted even more than love of one's God.

This was my world, and it fit me like a glove, except for the anger that was uniquely my burden. I secretly carried it with me, always lurking just below the surface. I held a secret disdain for the process and the participants.

There were periods when I thought I had conquered it and times when I thought I would die from it. It reached a critical stage when Grandma Nina passed away in my senior year in college. I resented God for taking her from me. I missed her English accent and her warm, quiet nature. Her strength and her belief in me were my life's blood. Her death left me empty, and I filled the space with vile resentment.

I never knew when the venom would fill me. There were so many things that triggered it that I would have found it very difficult to pinpoint which stimulus was most potent. A perceived insult or snub would send me into a frenzy of frightening, vengeful thoughts. Bloody images of the object of my anger would flood my mind. I was on a collision course with disaster, and I knew it. I never bothered to count the many times I was guilty of feeling superior to another person because of my achievements or some other meaningless conceit.

Even though I knew intellectually that I was suffering from an emotional disorder caused by my early years, the burden of carrying the monster with me was exhausting and, when stimulated, it was almost uncontrollable. I was forced time after time to hide behind my smiling mask and ride it out. The hard part had always been hiding it.

I often wondered if my father before me was a victim of overwhelming anger as I was, or if he was simply the cruel monster I knew him to be. It was reasonable to assume that my problem was a product of the abuse I had suffered as a child, and I wondered, only occasionally, if Pops had suffered abuse when he was a boy. My hatred for him colored my existence; thinking of him as a victim was torture.

Once, when I found myself wondering if he was also a victim, Franny suddenly voiced her opinion. "You're going to tell me that son-of-a-bitch was a friggin' victim now?" she growled. "You never had to deal with the dirty bastard, and now you're going to feel sorry for him?" Franny was becoming a problem. I hadn't worked this hard only to have her wreck my chances to escape that life.

"Silence, Franny!" I told her. "Go away! My name is Faye. That's right ... Faye Lawrence. No, I'm sorry I don't know you ... but I must say ... I'm not fond of your vulgar language."

Chapter 20

Uncle Paul's life was altered by our needs over and over again. This time, it was my brother Willie who strayed. He was picked up for drinking while driving and disorderly conduct. Uncle Paul had to fish him out of the local jail in the middle of the night. Paul wasn't a man who held a grudge for an honest mistake, but he also wasn't a man who took mistakes that involved the police lightly either.

"Willie," he said, "you've disappointed me tonight. Why did you do this? You can decide a fair punishment for yourself. One that fits your ... shocking behavior and one that will serve you as a reminder not to repeat it in the future ... Get it?" he grilled his nephew.

"You can get back to me in two weeks, Willie," Paul instructed. "Until then, you can spend the time thinking about it." With that, he strode up the stairs, and Willie could hear his door close softly.

When I heard about the problem with Willie, I couldn't help but remember the ride home from school so many years ago when a frowning Chucky had warned me that Willie could say "fuck" any time he wanted to. It brought a smile to my lips that I couldn't resist. I loved my sweet brothers and often wondered if they would be sweet in adulthood—or if they had inherited the unthinkable, too.

Willie had inherited a lot of my mother's easygoing personality, and her intellect as well, but his heart was good and more than made up for any intellectual lacking he may have had.

I knew Willie was just trying to fit in. All he wanted was to have people like him, so he went with the crowd. I thought that maybe Uncle Paul could have been more supportive.

Willie adored Paul, and I knew he would be heartbroken to have disappointed him. He had known real punishment unlike any that Paul could have imagined. So now what would he choose?

Before the two weeks went by, Willie came to Paul and told him that he was having a problem selecting a punishment that would satisfy both of them. Uncle Paul thought it would not build character to let Willie off the hook too easily, so he told him he would have to go back to the drawing board. The challenge he gave Willie would come back to haunt Paul for the rest of his life.

He was disappointed when Willie didn't come and talk to him about his punishment after the two weeks were up, but he didn't place much importance on it because he thought that Willie was trying to avoid facing him.

Paul had planned that the worry Willie would experience concerning his punishment during those two weeks would *be* the punishment. He felt quite clever for devising this unique torture, and he was anxious to tell Willie that all was forgiven. He had given some thought to a lecture he would give Willie about the dangers of drinking and driving. Paul had also decided that Willie should be held responsible for restoring the damage he had caused by working off the payment for his fine and the damage he had caused to some stop signs in Fenwick.

The problem with Willie was that he blamed himself for the unbearable conduct of his father, and alcohol eased the pain. He found acceptance and comfort inside a drug-induced fog. It was a cruel twist of events that denied Paul the pleasure of seeing Willie mature into the man he thought Willie could be. It would be one of many sorrows that our family brought into Paul's life.

When Paul went to confront Willie, all he found was a note saying that Willie was sorry for everything. Beside it was a small package wrapped in a handkerchief and secured with a rubber band. When Paul picked it up, it felt as though there was nothing in it.

"Oh Lord, don't let this be a used hanky," he muttered. It turned out it was not a dirty hanky; there was something inside, and when Paul saw it, he staggered back in disbelief. Staring in horror, his face ashen, he gasped, "Willie! Willie! What have you done?"

The note inside read:

Dear Uncle Paul,

This is the end of my little finger. I cut it off in the mower. Please bary it in a place where I can be baried when I die. Your soul can't rest if all your parts ain't in your grave when you die.

I'm sorry I didn't find a punishment that would be good but I can't think of it now. Me and Ralph we are going to join the Marines if they want us. I'm sorry for what I did. Tell them all goodbye.

Willie PS. Don't lose my finger.

One ill-conceived incident had snatched him away before Paul could help him. Paul was overcome with remorse and guilt. "My God, my God! What have I done? This is my doing!" he said.

When Uncle Paul told me about it, I felt my heart would break, and what hurt me most of all was that Willie had picked up his belongings and banished himself in shame. That's when I saw my opportunity to punish Paul. "Please don't feel bad, Uncle Paul," I sympathized, "he was already damaged when he came to you. Willie was abused ... he knew life wasn't always fair. You shouldn't blame yourself. We all do things that are, well ... mean-spirited ... from time to time."

I could hear the stunned contrition in his voice then, and the monster in me rejoiced. *You and your stupid sister, you're both the same. When you were needed most, you turned your face away.*

I knew that he wasn't mean-spirited, but I was in pain thinking of my brother's absence. I wanted to punish someone for it, and Uncle Paul was an easy target because of his gentle nature and because he cared so deeply.

He never gave up on Willie. He kept looking for him and trying to bring his nephew home, but Willie had an appetite for his new friends and the wild life. He felt accepted, even needed by them. Could Paul have made things different if he had given Willie absolution on the evening the boy came to him, eyes cast down, asking for help? Paul would always wonder.

Willie, Willie, my sweet brother! Where have you gone?

Chapter 21

My first job after receiving my degree in law was in the newsroom at KADN, a local television station in Fargo. It wasn't my first choice, but I took the job until I could get the right job in my field. I liked it because there were no hard and fast rules and, as a reporter, I could move around freely and compose my own schedule.

There were three journalists in our office. Martin Jacobson was the older of my two co-workers. I thought he must be in his late thirties or early forties. He was an average-looking man with red hair, and he wore glasses. He was stocky and pleasant-looking.

Kenneth Murphy was younger, maybe in his late twenties or early to mid-thirties. He was elegant, dressing in expensive-looking clothes that were always a perfect fit and always in excellent taste. He was a little taller than average, with dark brown hair and blue eyes. He was attractive and a pleasant conversationalist.

I made up the rest of our little team. We were the journalists. I had difficulty adjusting to some aspects of this environment.

I was especially irritated by my two male co-workers constantly referring to me by one endearing name or another. It was obvious that neither of them took things too seriously.

It was hard to be too formal in a three-person office, but one thing that I could not abide was all the overly familiar pet names I was lavished with. I found it demeaning no matter how well-intentioned. I wanted to be taken seriously, I wanted to be successful.

"Tell me, did I ever say my name was Sweetie Lawrence?" I asked. "No, I believe I remember saying that my name is Faye … Faye Lawrence. Could you remember that please?" I asked.

"Sure, but could you promise not to call me Kenny? I prefer Mr. Kenneth," one of them said, and they both laughed.

I joined them in spite of myself; I felt camaraderie with the two of them for their guileless acceptance of me. I loved being around them. I felt some unexplainable warmth about them that I enjoyed.

I considered myself as qualified as them in every respect. My title was the same as theirs, and I was not happy with that. I didn't want to be a small cog in a big wheel. I decided that I had to change this arrangement as soon as possible. *I, after all, am an attorney,* I thought. I started to make my plans immediately. I smiled inwardly at the prospect of going toe to toe with these silly innocents. They would never know until it was too late that complacency is not rewarded in the workplace.

I began my campaign by endearing myself to these two flirty, carefree guys, cheerfully running errands for them as though it was a privilege. I stood to gain very little by doing this, except to convince them both that I was not competing with them for an upcoming promotion soon to be awarded.

The supervisor of our area would be retiring, and I reasoned that one of us would get the job. I hoped they would let their guard down, and I could slip up unnoticed and overcome them. I still had the arrogance of a new graduate. The problem was that along the way, they became my friends, and I treasured them.

Success came quickly for me at KADN. Knowing that the tactics I used weren't completely scrupulous, I justified it all by playing the feminist card. The end justified the means in my mind. Who could forget those demeaning names? Not me!

Once I was promoted and became their boss, I sent my two friends to sensitivity training to reinforce my request that they refrain from unwelcome familiarity. They both accepted this rebuff with good-natured contrition. I was truly impressed by them both and their generous spirits. I was glad they were my friends. They were, after all, my first and only friends outside the family.

The first official thing I did was to recommend a raise for the two of them, maybe to make amends for playing unfair in order to get the promotion. It didn't matter, it was long overdue anyway. They were both too talented to be stuck in the pay scale they were in. I often wondered why they didn't find something more deserving of their talents.

"Thank you, Mzzz Lawrence," Martin said.

"Please," I answered, "call me Faye."

"Sure thing, Faye," Kenneth said, throwing me a kiss.

"Do you need another training session?" I asked.

"I'm already wearing ladies' underwear," he said, grabbing his chest as though he had breasts.

"You're excused," I said, motioning the chortling two-some out of my cubicle. I felt a guilty pleasure at having bested them, like an athlete who had vanquished someone who was both a friend and an opponent. It was bittersweet, but more sweet than bitter.

We began to meet at the Moon Café sometimes for lunch, sometimes for dinner and drinks, or sometimes just for drinks after work. It was fun and comfortable, and I always looked forward to those times. Most of the time I controlled my anger easily, and life was going smoothly. I wondered if I finally had it under control.

Finally I was on my own completely, with my own apartment and car, my own job, and best of all, my privacy. I loved the anonymity of this lifestyle. I loved the little coffee shop I frequented just a little way from my apartment. I could easily walk there in the morning for my breakfast before work, and I often stopped there on my way home for the warm ambience it had.

The biggest problem in my life at this time was Franny; she was cropping up from time to time out of the blue. She was showing up more frequently than usual, bringing her filthy memories and self-pity with her. One evening after work I stopped at my coffee shop for the warmth of some conversation and a burger. I was shocked that Franny appeared suddenly.

I paid my bill and left before she could embarrass me. How dare she approach me here on my own turf? She followed me home that evening, whimpering in my ear about her problems.

How I hated her pitiful little face telling her horror stories in that disgusting broken English of hers.

"I don't even know who you are," I told her, "and believe me, you don't know who I am. It happens that my name is Faye … That's right, love, I'm Faye Lawrence. You could never go where I have gone, never enjoy the comforts of decency I have. Why? Because you are now and always will be a child of incest, nothing more!"

I was filled with the blackest rage when she questioned my identity. "You're nothin' but a Goddamned phony, that's what," she charged. "You wanna be somethin' you're not … you're nothin' but a phony whore!"

I didn't stop at my coffee shop the next morning because I was late getting started, and I was afraid someone had noticed Franny. I got into my car and drove directly to work, no breakfast.

I dreaded these encounters with her, and I always wondered, "Will this be the one battle I can't win?" This was the one thing that brought me to my knees in prayer. "Please Lord, help me now. I'm afraid that I'm lost!"

I needed to forget Franny and these crazy episodes I was suffering with her, so I threw myself into my job even more intensely in the weeks and months that followed. I didn't dwell on problems I had with my past as much when my mind was busy with other things. That was the best way for me to deal with her.

I kept myself running in every direction and working additional hours late into the evening. I could keep her at bay that way. I am a preparation freak anyway, always needing to know why, where, and how, no matter what the project. It's a natural tendency of mine. So working late helped me, and the nights Martin, Kenneth, and I met for dinner or just drinks helped. Conversations with the two of them were always engaging and fun.

I have a highly developed instinct regarding human interactions, an uncanny ability to know exactly when to fight for what I want and when diplomacy is best. Even though I was still a relatively young woman, this talent was developed over many years of surviving the situation I was born into.

I displayed my knowledge of the business whenever I could, discreetly but unmistakably, to those who could benefit me in any way. My efforts soon caught the eye of those who breathed the rarified air of authority and power.

At this time, it was becoming more and more fashionable to speak with an accent in the world of media, especially a British accent. Many movie stars mysteriously became unable to speak without a British accent, and many commentators used this affectation to enhance their image. I knew the feeling well. I loved my British ancestors and modeled every syllable after theirs. I had chosen to speak as they spoke when I was still a child.

I was soon noticed for my work and also for my accent. I was interviewed and offered a temporary anchor position at KADN. This would be a trial position. I had a six-month period in which I could prove my ability to handle it or be demoted. The pay was very appealing. It was a tempting offer.

It seemed that time passed at warp speed, and suddenly the day arrived when I would co-anchor the evening news. I felt unprepared, even though I had thoroughly studied the material the station provided me. Would the audience think I was pretty? I had never thought of myself any other way. I knew I was pretty, but would I have the right look? Would I be accepted by the viewing audience?

Another thought I entertained too often was the last talk I had with Franny. I wondered if I would be perceived as a phony. Would my beloved accent suddenly leave me? "Hello, my name is ah … Fra … I mean Faye Lawrence, and I'm fillin' in fer … … aaah … fer ya know, what's-er face … Oh my God!"

I started to perspire, and when I looked at my hands they were shaking a little. Just then, Kenneth and Martin stepped into my office.

"If you get nervous out there, darlin', just think of me naked," Martin said.

"And if that doesn't work, think of me," Kenneth laughed. "I'm wearing ladies' underwear!"

I ran to them. "Thank you, thank you both," I cried and threw myself into their arms.

"Don't worry, Faye, they're going to love you!" Kenneth said, pulling me close. I could smell his clean skin and feel his breath in my hair. "What's not to love?" he said into my hair.

Time! The producer called and I was going on the air. I took one last frantic look in the mirror before I took my seat. *What's not to love?* I thought.

Once seated, the producer held his hand up counting "three … two … one" and pointed at me.

"Hello, my name is Faye … Faye Lawrence, in for Jane Timberlake."

Chapter 22

My debut was successful, but I was disappointed because the position wasn't offered to me on a permanent basis immediately. I didn't have the stomach for suspense, but I agreed to continue with the position on a trial basis as we had agreed for the time being.

My background was in law, not journalism, and that concerned me. I was sure that this would be considered before the job was offered permanently. I was reassured when the station began receiving comments from the viewing public. Most of them were complimentary, and some of them even contained words like *wonderful* and *professional*.

I was thrilled that there were only a couple of negative comments among all those positive ones, and they weren't about me specifically as much as they were opinions about news items we had reported. There were letters commenting on my "exotic" looks, my accent, and even asking if I was born here in the U.S.

I was feeling a little claustrophobic because of the letters questioning my origins, and I had no desire to delve into my past. I decided that I was going to have to quell the curiosity by answering the letters personally. I grabbed the mail from the box on my desk as I left the station. I decided I would respond to them at home that evening at my leisure.

The mail was uncomfortable to carry, and I wished that I had taken the time to put the letters in my briefcase. I walked to my car holding the mail and thumbing through it absentmindedly in the gathering darkness. To my surprise, I realized that I was looking at a letter from the county prosecutor's office.

I had interviewed with that office before I applied at KADN. I had taken the job at the station as my second choice while I waited for something to open up in my field. I had checked back once to see if I was still in the running, but that was a little while ago so I had put it out of my mind for the time being. Curiosity got the better of me, so I sat down on a bench at the bus stop and opened the letter under the dim streetlight above.

Dear Faye Lawrence,

Thank you for your letter informing this office of your continued interest in the prosecuting attorney's position.

Our records show that your area of expertise meshes perfectly with the requirement for a position opening within a few months in this office.

If you are still interested in a position here you may contact this office to schedule an interview.

Best regards,

Michael O'Leary

Michael O'Leary wanted to know if I was interested in a position in his office! My heart skipped a beat. I remembered him because I had been attracted to him. He was handsome, clean-cut, virile, and well-spoken. His long lanky body was languid and self-assured. I had thought of his lips briefly, but soon forgot them when he hadn't made an effort to meet me socially—plus, I didn't know his marital status. That was before I knew that Kenneth was … the way he is, anyway, so I was no longer interested.

I had worked hard for this opportunity, but now that it was here I asked myself, *Do I want to give up this comfortable existence I have built for myself to go fight the demons that beleaguered me in my childhood?*

I decided that I would think about it later, in the quiet of my own home. Maybe I would call Kenneth and Martin when I got home to see what advice they could give me. I thought of Kenneth, of how he smelled. Yes, it would be a good excuse to call them, I thought.

Clutching the letter, I stuck the rest of the mail under my arm, hung my bag on my shoulder, and hurried to my car thinking a million thoughts. The feeling of Kenneth's embrace was in the mix. This was a dream all right, but now I had some decisions to make. Do I follow my lifelong dream, or do I go for a career at the station and stay near Kenneth? I hurried to my car and threw my junk, all except for the letter from the prosecutor's office, across the driver's seat into the passenger's seat.

Out of the blue a chill swept over me and I felt exposed for some reason, my ears pulled back reflexively flattening themselves against my head, the hair on my arms stood erect, the skin beneath it crawling, a familiar stench wove its way into my consciousness; I felt the breath that carried it ruffling my hair, "Who's there?" I whimpered urgently, I couldn't turn and look, I was paralyzed with fear, "Who's there?" I cried, my heart pounding so loud I could hear nothing else just the pounding and a voice shouting, "G-O-D!" as though he had promised to watch my back but had fallen asleep. I recognized that voice …it was mine!

Before the sound of his name died on my lips, a hand shot out, grabbed the back of my hair, yanking my head back sharply. *Oh, no! Please God, no more!!*

"Keep yer Goddamn mouth shut, er-al shut'er fer ya!" a voice breathed close to my ear. I felt my precious letter slip from my fingers and float to the walkway. My memory went into overdrive. I had buried most of my past deep in my subconscious awhile ago. I wanted it to stay buried forever, but now those deeply guarded secrets of mine roared back, taking control of my psyche. No mercy!

The unvarnished truth reclaimed its place in my mind, and an indescribable loathing washed over me. I was plunged into the crushing memories of my sordid past.

Now something very dark and frightening was awakened within me. I feared it, but I didn't resist it. I felt the dark power of hatred, and I was seduced by it. It was my monster awakened after all this time, an old friend … here to help me through the hard times!

I had been trained well, before memory caught me, to separate myself from the physical abuse that my body endured and to watch from somewhere safe. I had learned how to tap the power of an undiluted form of hatred, purer than any the evil one himself ever served up.

"You don't know who you're dealing with, Pops," I warned. "You're not going to have much fun this time."

He answered by throwing me across the driver's side seat into the passenger seat, then climbing in behind me he smashed his fist into my face as he had done so many years ago. I made no response. He got nothing!

My dark companion and I watched from a safe place. I felt it growing stronger, fed by the purest form of undiluted hatred that ever existed.

"That was a big mistake, old man," I said softly.

"Gim-me them keys, we're gun-na go see Mama. The other lye-n bitch!" he said.

"Are ya gunna tell my mama on me?" I taunted him, remembering his threats from years ago.

"Shut yer fuckin' mouth or al kill ya here! Git them God-damned keys. Now!" he bellowed, grabbing my hair and twisting it until I felt some of it give way.

"They're in my bag," I said evenly, not giving him the pleasure of seeing my pain. I picked my bag up. *I've pushed the rotten pervert too far,* I thought.

He came back for revenge on my mother and me because we sent him away to prison. He means for both of us to die tonight. No need to rush that!

Wait ... wait for the right time! my dark companion cautioned me.

Remembering the pact my mother and I had made the night he was arrested, I knew exactly what I must do, and I was prepared to do it. I wondered how he had gotten out of jail. Was he paroled, or had he escaped? If he had escaped, it would mean the police were looking for him.

The downside to that scenario was that any police action would probably expose my ugly past, and also whatever he had planned for my mother and me would have to be completed in haste, before the police could find him.

I looked at him for the first time since he had intruded on my life again. It seemed that oceans of time and space separated me from my old tormenter, and yet I was still bleeding and sore. My heart was as black as the inside of that dreaded boxcar I feared as a child.

His hair had lost the blue-black highlights it once had, replaced by a lusterless salt-and-pepper gray. A new scar ran from his left eye down his cheek, ending at the corner of his mouth. A cigarette dangled from his mouth unlit, bobbing up and down as he talked. *Jail must be a tough gig,* I thought.

I was not moved; I had some scars of my own. My life has been virtually without childhood joys or youthful romance because of him. He gave me adulthood before I had childhood or adolescence and left me suspicious, cold, and filled with hatred. I was tiny, and he abused and beat me. My hatred for him, the filthy pervert, was almost unbearable. The most sophisticated measuring devise ever invented could never quantify the magnitude of the hatred I held for him! It consumed me!

Look pathetic for someone else, old man, someone who gives a damn! the monster whispered from somewhere deep.

"Hello, my name is Faye ... Faye Lawrence," Pops mimicked, and then he bellowed, "Yer fuckin' name is Franny and yer last name is Beck, same as mine! Who in hell do ya think ya'ar?" His eyes were wild now. He was working himself into a rage so that he would be justified in whatever little surprise he had in store for me. He wanted to establish the fact that no matter what happened, it was I who had forced the issue; he had no part in it, he was victimized by me! ... Ah, sweet memories!

I wanted to strip him of his alibi. I didn't want to supply him with an excuse for murdering me. "It's just a stage name, Pops," I consoled him gently. "The station prefers it, and I needed the job." I felt the power of total separation from this scene now, and I watched from a safe place. I had to check and see if I had any power over him. I looked for a vulnerable place, somewhere to start an assault.

I found the keys in my bag and held them out to him. He eyed me as though he was contemplating whether he should kill me on the spot or wait until later.

"I had a long time ta think about you. Oh yeah! You an that good fer nuthin', brain-dead whore a-yers. The way ya turned on me fer nuthin. Yer gun-na pay now. Yer gun-na pay big ... Faaaaaye!" he sneered.

"Yes, I know Pops, Mom turned on me too," I confided. "I can take you to her," I volunteered, making my voice sound childlike.

He turned and eyed me in that cunning way of his, as if he were deciding my fate. Weighing what I had said. *Oh, yes ... I'm in charge now, old man*, I thought. I saw that his eyes had that certain look, that look of liquid, I recognized that from my childhood, and I smiled at him. I had discovered his soft underbelly, and I felt my strength growing.

Two points of vulnerability: his hatred of Mom and his sexual obsession for his daughter ... after all these years ... sad bastard!

I knew now that there was very little time left for talk. Fortunately, the sound of laughter caught his attention as a young couple walked by, holding hands and chatting. They drew his eyes away from me, and a tiny window of opportunity presented itself.

I seized the moment and slid my hand into my bag, palming my hair spray. Turning it so that the nozzle was facing out, I held it in my hand with my pointer finger poised over the spray trigger, obscured from his view.

Take your time, take your time, the monster whispered. *If he tries anything, then let him have it. Spray his eyes until he's blind, and don't stop till the dirty bastard begs for mercy!*

He started the engine and began to back the car out, turning his face toward me to peer out the back window. He arched his body, fishing in his pocket for his lighter as he drove.

Take you time ... use your head, the dark one cautioned.

"Yer both gun-na be dead before they know," Pops vomited with his foul breath, his cigarette bobbling.

Holding my breath, I waited to see what would happen next. He ignited his lighter and brought it to his cigarette, puffing to draw the flame in.

NOW! the monster shrieked. *DO IT!*

I deftly drew my hairspray and sprayed directly over the flame and into his face in a continuous spurt. It ignited like a blowtorch. The flames licked his face, his hair started to burn and melt. He opened the car door and tumbled out, bawling like a wounded animal.

I leaped into the driver's seat and cranked the wheel to right the car as it meandered off course. I felt a bump ...

bump, under the front tires as they rolled over something, but I didn't stop or look back. I knew what it was.

"Have a light, Pops," I said as I drove away. "Burn in hell!" Ha!

Part Four

Chapter 23

I drove directly to a drive-through car wash. Whirling soft brushes caressed my car; water flowed, squirted, and pounded against it. I sat inside desolate, alone, hopeless, and damned.

"I'm going to hell," I whispered. *If he dies, I've murdered him, and I can never change that,* I thought. My heart felt like lead in my chest. I was filled with foreboding on so many levels. I thought of my job, my comfortable life, my respectability, and my soul.

My fear of this lunatic was thick enough to cut with a knife, but the way I hated him frightened me even more.

The dark and evil thing that had inhabited my psyche was small now and had fallen asleep. It's crazy how remorse can move right in and snatch away your evil power, just when you think you're totally immune to the constraints of civilized society.

I was crushed now, so I called Kenneth and Martin. Kenneth answered, and I was glad it was him. The sound of his voice was ambrosia to me.

"Yeah, what's up?"

"Are you busy, Kenneth? You must meet me at the Moon Café."

"What's wrong, Faye?"

"I have a problem," I sniveled, my voice breaking a little.

"Honey ... I mean Faye! What's the matter?" he asked.

"Someone jumped me at my parking place. I think I may have killed him."

"What! My God, shut up! We'll be right there ... blessed Father." Kenneth's deep baritone voice was suddenly not so deep.

It seemed like an eternity passed before Kenneth and Martin slowly pulled up in Kenneth's black Mercedes. They parked at the curb and stepped out, looking around for me almost sneakily, as though a throng of police officers was about to swarm them.

I stepped out of the shadows behind them shaking my head. "Maybe calling you was not the best option," I said as they turned around to greet me.

"That's not funny. Is this a joke?" Kenneth asked, laughing. His hair was still wet from his shower.

"It's not a joke, Kenneth," I said.

"Get in the car," Kenneth said. "We have to talk!"

"Listen to me!" I said, struggling for control. "The first thing we have to do is drive to my parking place. I want to see if he is dead or not."

"Jesus, Faye, what do you mean *dead?*" Kenneth asked. His eyes searched mine for an answer. "Blessed Jesus!" he corrected himself.

"Please just drive me to my parking place. I don't want to take my car because there may be a witness, and I could be recognized by someone."

"A witness?" Kenneth asked in sort of a yelled whisper. "What do you mean *witness*? What did you do that they could witness?"

"Well … Oh my God, a man and a woman walked by just before I lit him on fire," I said, "and I don't know exactly where they were when he fell out of the car. Everything was going so fast at that point."

"Christ almighty, Faye … Shut up! Shut the hell up and start talking!" Kenneth's voice began to quaver as he covered his face with his hands. "Blessed Jesus," he corrected himself again.

Martin joined the interrogation: "You lit him on fire?"

"Yes! On fire."

"Was he in your car when you lit him up?"

"Yes! He was."

"Was he on fire when he fell, or jumped, out of your car?"

"Yes! Fell out … or I mean, he opened the door and tumbled out on purpose."

"Do you know the guy's name, Faye?"

"Why?"

"Okay. So you know who the guy is? So who is he, Faye?" Kenneth chimed in.

"Please let's go! I have to see if he *is* dead. Let's go now!" I begged. We drove the eight blocks to my parking place. As we approached, I could see nothing that would indicate that a crime had taken place there.

Fear stopped my heart when I saw there was nothing there, no flames, no police, no throng of people, no body writhing in flames. I contemplated what could have happened. Did he call out for help? Had the young couple stopped and helped him find his way to the hospital? Was he sighted, or had his eyes been burned away?

In all of this there was one fact that couldn't be denied: he had come here on a mission, and that mission was the destruction of my mom and of me, and he was still alive. I thought of my mother, legendary for her sweet naïve messages and calls. I loved her quirky little ways and the way she always kept me abreast of even the most insignificant family news.

Uncle Paul was once again going to be asked to help my family … I suddenly remembered a loan I had not repaid him. *He makes things too easy!* I thought.

"I'm going to have to get rid of the two of you for a minute, so I can make some calls," I told my two friends.

"Sure, okay," they nodded, glancing covertly at one another. "This is a joke, isn't it?" Kenneth chuckled. "You really had me going for a while, Faye."

They both laughed, "Oh crap! We've been had!" Martin said.

"I've never been more serious in my life," I told them. "I was attacked, and I can prove it. He slugged me in my mouth, can't you see it? If that doesn't convince you, go look at the smoke damage in my car."

Kenneth took my chin and held it up to the streetlight so that the light shined on it. "She's not kidding, Martin," he said. "Oh, no!"

Martin eyed me suspiciously. "You're not going to call that crispy critter, are you, Faye? If you're involved with the guy and you had some reason to burn him, we'll understand. You tell us why you did it and who this cat is to you. You tell us right now, so we know where you're coming from … If you're a victim, we're on your side, but if you're a cold-blooded killer … I'm not going to involve myself in any shenanigans …"

"Shut-up, Martin!" Kenneth cut in. "Who did this to you, Faye?" he asked.

"I don't know for sure who it was, but I suspect it's a man who has had a vendetta against my family for a long time because we were instrumental in having him jailed," I answered in half-truths. "I want to call my family and warn them that he is out of prison and looking for trouble."

"I think this is a matter for the cops," Kenneth offered.

Panicked now, I thrust my face into Kenneth's, pinching his arm hard for emphasis, "No police … No one … No one must ever know about this. Do you hear me? No one! If you tell anyone, I will be destroyed! Do you understand that?" I said vehemently.

They both stared back at me the way you would at some poor deluded lunatic in an asylum … completely incredulous. Turning my back on them, I dialed Uncle Paul and told him that "the fellow" we had testified against was out of jail and back for revenge. I asked him to watch out for Mom and told him that I had been involved in an incident with this person already this evening. For some reason, the telling of the story again brought on more tears, and I sniveled a little, feeling self-conscious as I did it.

"I'll drive up and fill you in tomorrow," I said.

"It sounds as though you are restricted in what you can tell me. Are you in trouble right now, Faye? Is Nick there?"

"I'm fine; I'm with friends, Uncle Paul. I'll talk to you tomorrow when I get there. I love you."

"Hold on, not so fast, Faye! You will talk to me now. I can't let you go without making sure you're truly with friends and not in trouble. Please put one of your friends on the phone, dear," he said, "Do it now!"

"Uncle Paul, please!"

"Put one of your friends on, Faye! Or I will call the authorities."

"Verify for Uncle Paul that I'm not being held hostage or something, please," I said and offered Kenneth the phone.

Kenneth looked confused and embarrassed but took the phone. "Hello, Mr. … Paul," he said, shrugging his shoulders and making a face. "My name is Kenneth Murphy."

"Well thank you, Kenneth. I do want you to know that we are dealing with a very dangerous man, and I appreciate your taking the care to help me out here. May I ask you how you came to know my niece?"

"I'm a fellow employee of Faye's and … a friend. She asked me to tell you that she's in good hands."

"Tell me, Kenneth, where is it that you work again?"

"Oh right, I work at KADN with Faye … for Faye, rather."

"Thank you, Kenneth, you've been a great help. It was a pleasure talking with you; perhaps we'll have occasion to talk again someday?"

"That would be nice, sir, thank you."

"Could I speak with my niece again, please?"

"Are you satisfied now, Uncle Paul?" I said taking the phone.

"Yes, he appears to be a nice young man. Answer this question with yes or no, Faye. Does he work with you at the station?"

"Yes, he does, Uncle Paul."

"Are you close friends, dear?"

"I'm going to hang up now. I love you, Uncle Paul."

"I love you as well, dear. Be careful and please don't stay alone tonight. Stay with your friends until we can figure this out."

We drove to the Moon Café to pick my car up and take it to my garage. Kenneth volunteered to ride with me just in case the "crispy critter," as he was known now, was lurking about.

We slid into the car to make the short drive. The smell of the hairspray and burned hair was unmistakable. There was fire and smoke damage on the roof of the car, but other than that there was no evidence of an attempted murder. Nonetheless, I made a promise to myself to get rid of the car as soon as possible.

"Looking at this and smelling the stench really brings the whole story to life," Kenneth said. "You weren't fooling when you said you lit him on fire, were you?"

"I wish I were fooling. This was one of the worst nights I've had in a very long time," I answered.

"More like the worst night you've ever had?" he asked, shaking his head in amazement.

"It certainly was," I answered, and I thought, *You will never know, my friend.*

Kenneth invited me to stay at his place that night, and I accepted gratefully. I was reluctant to stay at my apartment; I had the willies from everything that had transpired.

"Martin is a messy guy, so you'll have to put up with it. Maybe I'll get lucky and his wife will take him back soon," he laughed.

I had no idea if Pops had been stalking me for a while and knew where I lived, or if he had located my parking place by waiting unnoticed when I left my work and followed me to my car sometime before tonight. I felt certain that tonight wasn't the first time he had watched me from the shadows. I wondered absentmindedly if he had actually been in my apartment and if he had looked through my things like the criminal that he was. It actually depended, of course, on whether or not he was driving or was on foot. If he was on foot, he couldn't have followed me home because I always drove my car home from my parking place.

My friends and I talked into the night. I explained how it happened that I set fire to the intruder who tumbled from my car on fire and in agony. I was careful not to disclose his name or our relationship, even though both of them were obsessed with knowing. Kenneth and Martin were visibly awed by the hairspray caper, exchanging incredulous looks while I told them about it. Reminiscing about the events of this evening somehow made it seem a little easier to take.

We all tried to estimate how badly the intruder was hurt and how he could have crept away after being burned the way he was and run over by the car. They didn't know old Pops, or they would have known it was perfectly normal for him to have walked away. Indeed, I could visualize him standing in the shadows with his hair burned off and no brows or lashes, smoking his cigarette and staring at the windows of my apartment from the shadows, or maybe he was standing in some hidden nook watching us when we returned to the scene of the crime.

Bastard, I thought.

In the morning, a cold dawn washed the room in light, with hues of lightest blue. Guilt and doubt penetrated my awareness. Suddenly, attempted murder wasn't something to marvel at with friends. My head throbbed with a dull alcohol-induced ache. I was unquestionably an inexperienced drinker, and my low-grade headache and remorse reinforced my belief in abstinence. Everything seemed a little blue and too bright. I was anxious and filled with guilt.

Over and over again I reviewed exactly what I had told Kenneth and Martin. Had I spilled the beans somehow? What had I confessed to in my storytelling frenzy?

"My name is Franny ... that's right, Franny Beck. That's me. I'm the incest girl from the woods near Fenwick." Oh God! I'll be damned if I'm ready to switch roles with that pathetic little victim, I thought. "You are Faye Lawrence!" I said aloud. "Don't forget that!"

"I could never forget that, darling," Kenneth called from the kitchen, "and just to prove it, I have a cup of Joe and a couple of eggs with your name on them, whenever you're ready."

"Thanks, pal," I answered. The invitation perked me up somehow. I loved the sound of his voice. *I can handle this,* I thought. "I'll be there in a bit," I called. I picked my bag up and went down the hall to the bathroom. The first thing I noticed when I looked in the mirror was that my lips were swollen and discolored. I tested my teeth by wiggling them back and forth with my fingers to see if they were loosened. I had done this as a child, and the memory angered me again. They were still tight and looked normal. The reflection in the mirror looked back at me. "This is the last time that son-of-a-bitch will ever lay his hands on me," I told it. "I was justified in doing what I did to him, and if I did kill him, it was in self-defense."

Later at breakfast, Kenneth took my chin in his hand and looked at my bruises and my swollen mouth. He shook his head. "How can a man do something like this?" he asked. "How can he live with himself?" My body froze with desire for him, and I dropped my eyes so that they would not betray my secret. I told him how grateful I was that the two of them were in my life.

"You were lifesavers last night, and I'm so grateful to both of you," I said.

"You're our little firefly!" Kenneth said, avoiding my eyes as he cleared the dishes away. He was suddenly self-conscious; I liked that about him. Maybe he was hiding an emotion that he wasn't ready to share also. Quite honestly, I liked everything about him, and the feeling was growing.

"I thought you were going to call the station, firefly," Martin chimed in to take the edge off the moment.

"Indeed I was," I said as I rose from the table and gave Kenneth a hug. I wanted to cling to him, but I resisted and gave him an air kiss instead, inhaling and holding his fragrance. I called the station and arranged to take some time off. Fortunately, I had accrued several weeks of vacation time, and the station had been urging me to take it. The station frowned on hoarding time because it was difficult scheduling vacations so that everyone got their fair shot at the prime times.

Kenneth and Martin went with me to my apartment because they didn't want to chance having the "crispy critter" show up while I was there alone. I could see no evidence of anyone having been in my apartment except myself. I was happy to have them with me just in case I was being observed through some chink in the wall by the spiteful old jailbird. I threw a few things in a bag and prepared for my trip home.

I called Uncle Paul and told him that I was starting my drive home in the next hour or so, and that I should reach them by late afternoon or early evening. I didn't really welcome the drive, but I had no choice, and I did want to see my family anyway. I didn't want to leave Kenneth, though; for some unknown reason, I was becoming extremely enamored of him, and I thought that maybe it was just an emotional reaction to the ordeal I had just been through and all the old stressful memories that were stirred up. I could picture my mom making plans and preparing for my homecoming the way she always did, but I still didn't want to leave Kenneth. I loaded my stuff and gassed up my smoky-smelling car. My two friends were standing guard the way true friends would.

When I waved to them, they responded with a wave of their own, and I started to pull away.

No! I thought, *this is not enough,* so I stopped the car impulsively and ran back to them. The three of us stood there wondering what had just happened for a moment, and then I threw myself into their arms in a group hug.

It ended with me clinging to Kenneth for a little while, my face buried in his neck, inhaling his scent. He pulled me close; I felt his breath in my hair. "Call me," he whispered.

"I will, and you call me," I answered.

"C'mon," he said, taking my arm. We walked to my car. When our eyes met, he smiled at me and offered me his lips. I reached up to take them, and my heart burst into flame at the feel of his soft mouth. He opened the door and held my arm as I slid in. He pushed the door shut softly, and I watched him in the rearview mirror as I pulled away, standing with his hands pressing down in his pockets ... looking back at me. Everything was changed between us.

Chapter 24

I drove along, my mind reviewing what had happened, especially what had just happened and the events of yesterday. It seemed as if there were too many things to fit into one day. So many questions haunted me. Where was my attacker?

I flipped the radio on and found the news. I hoped to hear something that would tell me how he happened to be out of jail, if his injuries had come to the attention of the law or if he had been recaptured. What did he mean when he said, "Yer both gun-na be dead before *they* know?" Who was he referring to when he said *they*? Did he mean a member of the family or his jailers? *Know* what? That he was missing from his jail cell, or that he had fulfilled a promise he had made to *whom*, us or himself?

I wondered how long he had been out of jail and if he was well-established with a place to go, or if he was holed up somewhere under a bush or in an abandoned car. How bad were his injuries? Had he inhaled the flame? Lost his eyesight? Was he stalking my family at this very moment? Watching them with evil eyes from some hidden cranny?

I accelerated the car; the stench of his burned carcass filled the air, making me feel a little ill. An urgency to arrive at my destination and to see my loved ones again drove me forward into the familiar scenery of home. I finally came to the turn-off; I cruised by the school, past the post office, along the long drive with its white fence, and into the yard where my loved ones waited.

How grand it was to feel their flesh enfolded in my hungry arms. Phones are fine, but there is nothing like the human touch. It conveys more than words alone can say. There was one absence that hurt me to my soul, and that was my sweet brother Willie. I missed Chuck, who was away at school, but somehow it was different. Willie was my heart. He was deeply loyal, but he was vulnerable and loving. He wore his heart on his sleeve.

Chuck, on the other hand, was quick-witted and too handsome. He was almost secretive about his feelings and beliefs. He was self-contained and unapproachable when it served him. He was Uncle Paul's pride and joy. The breaker of many hearts, I'm sure.

The years Mom had spent here at her family home had transformed her from the agitated oddity she had become into the quiet loving mother she was always meant to be. I will confess that I felt the tug of jealousy seeing the interaction between her and Sharon again. Always touching! Looking at Sharon and her calm demeanor and obvious love for my mother, I have to admit I resented her. I guess I wanted to hurt her a little because she didn't have to share the bad parts of life in the Beck family. She was born a Lawrence; she never had to fight and claw to become a member.

There she stood with her auburn hair, her freckled skin that probably was never cold or bruised. She probably never had to check that broad smile of hers to see if her teeth were loosened. Yes, I felt like hurting her a little. I tried to hide my resentment when she came to me for her hug. "I love you, Faye," she murmured with her unbeaten face.

Then there was Uncle Paul. I clung to him for a while. How I loved him! "I'm glad you weren't hurt, Faye. I don't know what I would do if something were to happen to you. I love you, dear," he said softly with his British-sounding voice.

Patty, Paul's wife, waited for everyone to greet me before she did. She was so like Paul. I really loved her. They were a great couple. She was the type who everyone liked to spend time with … interesting and modest. Paul and Patty's boys were gone for the evening when I arrived, so I waited for morning to see them. The family listened intently when I told the story of the attack. How Pops had ambushed me when I went to my car and the whole story about the hairspray and his threat to Mom and me. None of us knew what we could do to combat another attempt on either one of us, or both of us.

"At times like this, it would be nice if our boys were home," Uncle Paul said, looking at Mom.

"It really would be. I could call Chucky and see if he could take the time away from his studies to come home for a while," Mom answered.

"No, dear, let's not think about that yet," Paul told her.

"One thing I definitely don't want to do yet is involve the police," I said. "I've worked too hard to escape my past life to have him ruin it for me."

"We'll try to handle it ourselves, Faye. The bobbies will be our last resort," Uncle Paul answered.

We stayed close together that night, listening to every cricket chirp with rapt attention. Leaves rustling in the breeze would silence conversation mid-sentence. I had forgotten about the deafening silence in the countryside. My ears had become so accustomed to the bustle of the city that the quiet of the country disturbed me. I finally dozed off as dawn broke. It was a fitful sleep lasting only a few minutes.

We were all well in the morning, and there were no sightings of anything out of the ordinary. The next morning the newspaper carried the account of a jailbreak. It stated that the police were conducting a manhunt for Nicholas "Nick" Beck, originally from Fenwick, North Dakota.

The story broke on the KADN morning news as well. So there it was. He was not paroled from jail, he had broken out. I felt exposed. Who knows how deep the station would dig for this story? Franny's name would certainly come up. The thought of what the fallout from this story might be brought me to my knees. "Please, dear God, protect me from being exposed. Protect me from my past."

My phone rang. It was Kenneth. "Speak to me," I said.

"Earth to Faye … earth to Faye," he answered.

"Ha! You're a funny man, Kenneth."

"Faye, I just had to ask you if Nicholas 'Nick' Beck is the crispy critter."

My heart stopped when I first heard that name. "Ha! Again, you're a funny guy. Why in hell would you ask me that? Leave it alone, Kenneth."

"I'm going to get a good look at him, and if he's missing his eyebrows, I'll know," he joked.

"Listen, Kenneth, I'm serious now. You must let this go. I insist that you vow on your honor that you will never tell anyone about Crispy Critter. Have you told anyone?"

"I have not," he answered.

"Then vow, right now."

"I'm sorry, I don't believe in making vows all over the place, so I won't vow … I never vow, but I can assure you I won't talk."

"Swear Martin to the same promise. Tell him he will learn to regret opening his mouth if he does … and Kenneth, I'm … well … sorry for pinching your arm. Are we good?"

"Totally!"

"How is everything at home?" I asked.

"Good, good," he answered. "Is everything all right there?"

"Nothing stirring here," I answered.

"All's quiet then?" he asked.

"So far it is," I said.

"Promise to keep me posted, no matter what happens. Won't you?" he pressed.

"I promise I will," I answered.

"Faye, do you ever think … you know, about … everything, I mean the last time we were together, how we were?"

"All the time, more than you'll ever know," I answered. "I do."

"Yeah?"

"Yeah," I answered.

"Am I saying too much?"

"Never!"

"That makes my day. May I call you again this evening?"

"That would be wonderful, Kenneth, if you don't mind. I'll wait for your call, so don't forget."

"Count on it, then. I'll call later. Say goodbye, love."

"Goodbye, love."

I missed being home. The phone call was a welcome diversion from the country quietude, but it was more than that. I closed my eyes and let my lips remember his ... *Kenneth, Kenneth.*

I decided that I would take a look around the outbuildings just to make sure none of them were "occupied." I walked around and through the outbuildings searching for clues that would tell me if we were being stalked, or a sign of some hiding place where someone had slept. Something like a cigarette butt discarded and left in sight. Pops had always pinched the embers from the end of his spent cigarette, leaving it flat with no ash at the burned end at all. I found nothing in the outbuildings and finally gave up my quest. I returned to the house feeling the fatigue of sleepless nights, but maybe slightly more secure.

We had dinner and listened to the evening news over our tea. We wanted to see if the escapee had been recaptured. We were disappointed to find that he was still at large. It was only a matter of time until Pops came for us. The only thing that would change that would be his capture or his death. If Uncle Paul or any member of his family was hurt because of my coming here, I would never be able to forgive myself.

These gentle people shouldn't have to barricade themselves in their home because of our problems. It was as though it never ended. One problem followed the other for us. It was as certain as the tide rises and falls.

Kenneth called after we had finished our dinner to say goodnight. "Faye?" he asked.

"Yeah, it's me, Kenneth," I answered.

"Faye, I'm having a tough time. I'm worried about you; have you had any news about Crispy?"

"Nothing at all," I said, "but I'll let you know if anything at all happens here. You'll be the first to know, I promise. Okay?"

"It seems so bizarre. You should have police protection," Kenneth said. "I don't like this at all."

"Do I have to pinch you again?" I answered.

"Ah … I remember well the very first pinch we shared."

"I said I'm sorry!" I protested.

"I could never forget a pinch so deftly delivered," he said smugly. "I hate to labor this … but I'm still in awe of that delightful little ditty … bestowed me; enhanced, as it were, with that nifty little twist added to the end … Ah, that little twist, that really put some life into it! But, notwithstanding the delight I took in receiving it, I must decline your generous offer to deliver another, since the thrill of the first still lingers," he laughed.

"Ha! You're a dead man, Kenneth, but you know that don't you?" I asked.

"I thought of you today, Faye."

"Me too, you."

"All day, every day … I'm going to hang up before I say too much. I'm kind of out of control since you left, Faye. I guess I'm worried about you. I don't know what's happening!"

"I think of your voice, Kenneth, of you, always."

"Yeah?" he asked softly.

"Yeah," I whispered.

"Say goodnight, love."

"Goodnight, love."

"Stay safe! And keep me posted."

"I will, don't worry," I said.

Kenneth's calls always filled me with romantic thoughts. I always had to take some time to recover after he hung up, going over every word in my mind to find evidence that he could truly love me.

The family slept an uneasy sleep that night as we had the previous night. Before breakfast was started, we listened to the news. Nothing had changed. He was still at large. "Yer both gun-na be dead before they know" played over and over in my brain. He had to mean that we were going to be dead before the prison knew he was gone. *Well, I'm sorry, Pops; you didn't make the deadline this time. They know you're gone!*

Chapter 25

Kenneth and I talked every day. He kept me posted on anything and everything at KADN, and I assured him every day that things were fine at my end. Four days passed; there was no evidence that the police were any closer to finding the slippery old convict, and there was also no evidence that he was hiding anywhere on the ranch. That was the day that Paul discovered a letter addressed to Franny Beck in the mail pile. He handed it to me. The postmark revealed that it was mailed in Fenwick. I opened the letter and read it:

Dear Franny,

Tell your sister to dress up and fix her hair. I am coming to see her.

Pops

I was stunned. I felt sick. He had fixed his sights on Sharon. I wondered if he even knew her name. He would love to strip her of her innocence. I wondered how he knew about her. He was imprisoned before Sharon was born—indeed, before my mother's physical changes from pregnancy even occurred. He hadn't even known she was pregnant. It could be, I suppose, that his attorney found out and told him ...

or could it be that one of the boys had been corresponding with him?

"I should have finished the job when I had the chance," I whispered. "He won't stop until one of us dies."

"He's on the move," Paul said when he read the letter. "He's letting us know that he is on his way. I'll have to call the police now, this has gone far enough," Paul said, giving me a look that said, *Don't say anything.*

I was adamant about not involving the police, but Uncle Paul was convinced that it was unfair to the other members of the family to endanger them by excluding the police. I still wasn't ready to surrender my anonymity, so I tried to entice Uncle Paul to give it another day or two.

"I'm sure he'll be caught before he can do anything crazy," I wheedled. "Using the U.S. Mail to threaten someone is a federal offense, Uncle Paul. It follows that if the police are called because of a letter I received through the U.S. Mail, the feds will be involved and then it could become big news very quickly. Interest in the story will certainly be all ramped up, and I'll be exposed."

"Yes … or we could be charged for withholding information that could lead to the apprehension of a dangerous escaped criminal," Paul retorted, exasperated. He looked at me coldly for a long time and finally sighed, "All right, two days," and quietly added, "and not a minute more."

"Thank you! Thank you, Uncle Paul," I cried, grabbing him in a fierce hug. He didn't resist, but he didn't respond to my hug either. I knew he was tiring of my grand deception.

"Not so fast, Faye, I am going to make a report to the police that we've had problems with him in the past. I won't disclose the letter, but I'm going to advise them that we've received a threat. That's the best I can do. You have to understand I have a responsibility to our whole family, more than to your anonymity. I refuse to gamble on their safety," he said.

"Okay, Uncle Paul," I conceded. I knew there was nothing more I could do to stop him. Those soft blue eyes of his had turned steely gray ... there was no changing his mind now.

I waited until I was sure everyone was sleeping and crept about the house like some spirit returned from the grave, checking this door and that closet with the stealth of an invader, peeping through the windows at the slightest rustling of leaves. I asked myself why everything always seemed worse during the night. Perhaps it's because, at night, there are fewer distractions, so that one has the time to indulge that part of the psyche that invites darker thought. Maybe most of us have some evil thoughts we struggle to suppress, and it's simply easier to suppress them when we have other things that are more pressing to override our baser instincts.

Finally, it was apparent that no matter what window or door I was patrolling, other windows and doors were unguarded. Stationing myself on the top step of the stairway where I could get a fair look at the entire hall in the upper portion of the house while keeping an eye on the main part of the living room was the best solution. The night seemed eternal. I was thirsty, and I wanted a glass of water, but I put off trekking down the steps to get it. *I'll rest for a while and then I'll run down,* I assured myself, *but first, I'll just sit here and keep watch for a while.*

"Wake up, Faye! Have you been here all night?" Mom was bending over me. I jumped to my feet, feeling a little contrite for sleeping at my post. "Go lay down before you fall down. I'll wake you later," she said.

"Just for a little while, Mom," I said. I was exhausted. "Wake me in an hour, Mom," I called.

"Sure, honey," she winked. "You can count on me." It was after nine when my mother finally woke me to tell me that, Mathew and Patrick were driving Patty to Montana and that they were all ready to leave. I showered quickly, dressed, and hurried down to join the rest of the family. Paul had decided that Patty would go to visit her sister in Montana until things cooled down. Paul would stay at the ranch to watch things. Paul didn't want to expose Patty to the dangers at the ranch and asked his son's to drive her. They were already hustling everyone into the car when I came down from my long nap.

I gulped a glass of milk and hurried out to help send Patty and the boys off. "I'll ride with you to the end of the drive," I volunteered.

"Sure, jump in," Patty said.

We went down the long drive with the white fence lining it on either side. It struck me how exclusive the place looked. How immaculately it was cared for. Patty stopped the car at the edge of the property, and I hopped out. I came around to her side of the car. "Have a great time with your sister, and don't worry about anything here," I told Patty. "Everything will be fine."

"Oh, I know, and thanks—we will have a wonderful time, I'm sure," she answered. I reached through the window and gave her a lopsided hug. Mathew and Patrick climbed out and hugged me, too.

"You guys have a good time," I said. They hopped in and were on their way. Looking down the road after them, I saw the mailman slowly approaching. I waved at him as he pulled up.

"Did your hired hand find your place?" he asked. "He wanted to catch a ride out here with me a few days ago, but you know, I can't let anyone ride with me because I carry the federal mail."

"Oh really, what did he look like?" I asked.

"Hard to say, I guess. He was big with fuzzy gray hair. His skin was sort of blotchy, come to think of it. He seemed a little weathered … I guess. He looked like he could do a good day's work though. Yup, he sure did!" he answered.

"So you didn't let him ride with you, then?" I fished.

"No, Jake Kramer came along, so he rode with him," the mailman went on. "I thought he would be here. He told me he worked with Paul every harvest; of course, you wouldn't know anything about him. He works out in the fields, I guess."

"No, he isn't familiar to me," I lied. "I'll ask Uncle Paul if he arrived safely." My eyes followed him as he slowly pulled away, touching his index finger to his forehead in the same one-fingered salute most of the natives in this area used as a greeting or parting gesture. As my eyes fell from his mail truck to the road below, I noticed there was a large round metal culvert running under the road to handle water drainage from heavy rains and snow when it melted in the spring.

The grass was bent on the shoulder of the road as though an animal … or something … had frequented the place. I had a bad feeling about this. It could be a place Pops would choose to hide. I was transfixed where I stood for a moment. I could run, I thought, but I realized that I had to check it out. I walked slowly toward the culvert, afraid I was being watched. One step and then another toward the culvert. Then I spied, by my foot, the very thing I feared the most: the familiar flat cigarette butt with its ember pinched off!

Turning on my heel, I started to walk rapidly toward the house with legs that were stiff with fear. Walking like a tin soldier marching down the road between the white board fences, toward the house on legs whose knees wouldn't bend. I felt eyes searing my back from some hidden nook as I marched along. Once there, I looked back and found no one ready to pound me senseless. The road was clear. I strained to see if he could be peering at me from the ditch, but again there was nothing there. I began to regret not having had the courage to peer into the culvert. I really wanted to know where he was—because if he wasn't in the culvert as I suspected, then where was he?

Have some courage, I told myself. *Go back and find out if he's in there.* I couldn't understand why I was so fearful now when I was the profile of courage before when he literally had his hand twisted in my hair. There was something about the unknown that was extremely frightening to me. Eyes that were unrestrained by a returning stare were free to take unlimited liberty with their prey.

If I did find him there, and he should come after me, how could I run fast enough to get to safety before he ran me down? It was the same fear that I'd known when I was the Christmas angel scrambling for safety and finding none.

Oh yes, this memory made my blood run hot. Now I felt the stirring of a different emotion, one I liked to refer to as the monster. It had been with me so long ago at Christmastime and gave me the courage to deny the bastard any response. It made me feel invincible, and I needed courage.

Off I went with my courage screwed up, on legs that were stiff with resolve and anger, marching back like a tin soldier, stiff and purposeful, to look in the culvert. When I got there, I approached it from the side that didn't show any sign of use. I reasoned he would be closer to the end that he used as an entrance, and I didn't want to be too close to him. I didn't want him to be able to put his filthy hands on me. Never again! When I looked in, he wasn't there. That meant that he was lurking in some hidden crevice, watching and waiting for his chance.

I crossed to the other side where a path was worn to the entrance. There were several flat cigarette butts scattered in it and a canvas tarp that he had obviously slept on and maybe used to keep warm on damp nights.

Chapter 26

It was finally obvious now that the police should be no-
tified of the threat we had received. We were all very much
in danger, and I felt responsible for us being unprotected. I
decided to call Paul and tell him about the find I had made
at the end of his driveway and to alert him about the "hired
hand" who had found a ride out here with Jake Kramer. I
was glad I had stuck my phone in my pocket in case Kenneth called me. I rang Paul's number, but he didn't answer.
I waited a few steps and tried again; no answer. I wondered
where they could be.

Hurrying up the driveway, I had a million different end-
ings to this dilemma playing in my mind. I was glad that we
had Uncle Paul here. I wanted to tell him what I had discovered and of the danger I had brought down on us by insisting
that he leave the police out of it. In spite of that, I decided
not to stop at the house when I reached it but continued
walking toward the barn, a huge red-and-white hip-roofed
two-story building, trying to reach Paul again as I walked
along with no luck.

Once there, I pushed the door open a little at a time from
the right side so I wasn't exposed completely. When nothing
happened, I gingerly stepped inside. It took a little while for
my eyes to adjust to the dim light in the building. A terrify-

ing little while! When I could see again, I looked for clues proving that someone had been there. A place that looked like it had been slept on, or walked on, or maybe a flat cigarette butt … his signature. After finding nothing on the first floor, I climbed the ladder to the upper floor where hay was stored to feed the animals in the winter.

There were places that showed evidence that an animal or a fowl had fashioned a nest in the hay to rest in, but nothing that looked suspicious.

There seemed to be a faint smell of cigarette smoke that lingered as I moved further to the rear of the hayloft. This convinced me that someone had indeed spent time here. I thought I might have found a place where a larger animal had found repose as I poked around. I knelt and sifted through the hay that seemed to have been disturbed, to see if there was evidence of him staying here.

While there on my knees, I noticed a shaft of light blazing down through a chink in the wall. I walked over on my knees and peeked out to see what, if anything, a sneaky old pervert could have seen while hidden here. I discovered that the house could be observed from here, along with all of the comings and goings of the family. The smell of cigarette smoke was oppressive when I put my face close to it.

Oh yeah! This was Pops all right.

I turned to go and my foot bumped something. I brushed the hay away and found a brown bag. Inside the bag I found an empty root-beer bottle that had been used as an ashtray, with several flat butts in it. He had been in our kitchen! There was evidence of food that he probably took from the kitchen as well. The place suddenly took a chill. If he had been in the kitchen, where else had he been?

Obviously, some very special plans were being made for the family, something unforgettable. I thought of the note he had written about Sharon, and I regretted my resentment of her. Pops had to know that this was the last opportunity for him. That whatever happened now was the conclusion of his relationship with the freckle-faced farm girl he had taken for better or for worse.

Yes, this would be something very special indeed. It occurred to me that maybe Willie and Charl, as Chuck referred to himself now, had kept us alive this long by their very absence. If I knew Pops, he would prefer to treat the whole family to his final tribute, whatever it was.

He probably waited and watched through the chink in the wall for them to come home. He would love to finish his business with Willie, anyway. I remembered how he had watched the boxcar the night he was arrested for assaulting Willie. God forgive me, but I did hate him relentlessly!

The odds that something devastating was about to happen to my family were overwhelming. I had to tell Paul what I had found immediately. I was afraid to climb down the ladder without first seeing who would be standing at the bottom of the ladder to greet me. I tried to peek into the lower level by sticking my head down through the small opening in the loft floor, but the structure surrounding the ladder was too deep, and there was no vantage point that would allow me to survey the lower level. Finally, I was forced to climb down the steps feet first, exposed to the unknown until I was far enough down to turn and look around the ground floor before I descended the rest of the way.

Once down, I moved with stealth across the huge floor, keeping my eyes busy checking here and there for any movement. I cautiously opened the door to the sunshine outside, blinded for a moment by the bright light, and then dashed toward the house and safety. I was relieved when I had the doorknob in my hand, but when I tried the door it didn't yield.

Something was blocking it. I pushed harder on the door and it gave way a few inches. Paul's arm flopped into my view. I felt a searing ache in my heart when I saw it and pushed the door open enough to squeeze through. Paul lay on the floor, blood oozing from his nose.

"Paul, my God, what happened?" I asked. I patted his wrist and cheek in an effort to revive him, but he didn't respond. I checked his heart. It was beating, and he was breathing. A lump was growing on his forehead, so I dashed into the kitchen and hurriedly started throwing ice in a bag.

Just then, an earth-shattering scream filled the air from the upstairs.

"Mom! A man!" Sharon screamed. Running feet, slamming doors, and Sharon's young voice screaming filled the house.

"Hello, ya rotten whore," I heard him bellow. "I cum-ta collect something from ya. I cum-ta git the girl here. She's a purdy one, Mama. I'm gunna kill ya and take-r. Ha!"

"Take your filthy hands off her!" I heard my mother boom. "Let her go!" Her voice was raspy with emotion.

"Ha! What are ya gun-na do with that? Shoot me? Go ahead shoot! C'mon shoot!" He taunted. "You'll never git-er back, ya dirty bitch. I waited a long time fer this, now yer gunna pay. She's mine now ... Understand?"

"Let her go, Nick," Mom warned, her voice quavering. I bolted up the stairs three at a time. I reached the top of the stairs just as two gunshots rang out. I leaped into Sharon's bedroom with my heart in my throat. Nick slithered across the floor toward me on knees and elbows, rolling and crawling in a diversionary tactic, leaving a trail of blood as he went.

I recoiled in horror as he approached me. He looked like a lizard as he crawled close to the floor in this hideous posture to escape her bullets. He crossed the floor and slithered out of the bedroom; then rising from the floor, he loped down the stairs and out of the house, bleeding as he went.

Mom's face was expressionless. It was a look I had seen before. She stood in shocked disbelief, hugging Sharon's head to her shoulder with her left arm while her right arm hung limply, dangling the gun at her side until it finally slipped from her fingers and clattered to the floor.

A translucent veil of blue smoke churned in the warm morning sunlight and became invisible in the shadows. Her eyes found mine, holding them for a few moments, reliving our painful history together. I could feel the icy waters of the mighty Mouse River under her gaze, and I knew what I must do. I remembered the vow we had made to each other when I was a child.

My mother and I were thrown together now in the same struggle we had lived with for most of our lives, and now we shared a profound remorse that the problem we had solved so long ago wasn't solved at all. I thought of Paul downstairs on the floor in the foyer. Mom and I walked Sharon down the hall to Mom's room.

"Stay here," I told them, "and don't come out until I come and get you."

"We will," they said in unison.

"Lock the door and don't open it," I said.

I closed the door and ran down the stairs to make sure Pops was really gone; after satisfying myself that he was, I went to see if I could help Uncle Paul. He was still lying motionless on the floor. This is not good, I thought. He really needs medical attention. I realized then that I had to get him help, even if my precious identity was destroyed.

After I called the emergency number and asked for an ambulance, I called Patty to tell her that I had found Paul unconscious on the floor.

"Just to be on the safe side, I called an ambulance," I told her.

"What?" she yelled. "What happened?"

"I don't know; I found him on the floor. Maybe he fell or something," I lied.

"I need to come home," she said.

"I've called the ambulance, Patty, so there really wouldn't be much more you could do right now. He's in good hands. Let's keep a good thought until we get more from the doctor."

"I really think I should come home, Faye."

"Look, Patty, I know you're worried about Paul, but I don't want the three of you driving all night. If something would happen to you and the boys, think what would happen to Paul then. Think of Paul. Why not let me call you as soon as I talk to the doctor. There is really no logical reason for you guys to jump in your car and start driving. I'm sure it's nothing critical anyway," I said.

"I don't like this," she said. "I just have a bad feeling about it." I could hear that she was crying.

"Patty, we're going to have to go to the hospital right now, but I will call you the minute I get anything."

"Thanks, Faye, I'll be waiting. Oh, by the way, have they found … you know … him?"

"Not yet," I lied.

"Could he have done this to Paul?"

"No, Patty, not a chance!" I hung up. I felt lousy. "I've had my fill of lies, but I can't have her hanging around here until this business with Pops is resolved," I whispered.

The ambulance came and the medics examined Paul. He was conscious now but not talking much, just an occasional yes or no.

"He seems fine," they said after a few preliminary tests. "We'll take him in. I think they'll want to check him over just to make sure everything is normal and check that nasty bump on his head. Okay?" they asked.

"Sure," I answered. "We'll follow you in."

Chapter 27

As soon as they started to head down the long driveway, I grabbed a scrub bucket, filled it with water and bleach, and dashed up the stairs, grabbing a towel from the bathroom. I frantically cleaned the bloodstains from the floor with bleach water. When I had the blood cleaned up, I surveyed the room, looking for evidence of a violent confrontation. I saw none … except for the gun. I stuck it in my belt and pulled my shirt out to cover it. I told Mom and Sharon that we were going to follow the ambulance to the hospital. They were stunned.

"Ambulance?" Mom asked.

"Yes, I called an ambulance for Paul," I answered. "Maybe Sharon should splash some cold water on her face; it's really red and blotchy from crying," I told her, trying to avoid whatever scene was about to unfold.

"Ambulance?" Mom's voice was becoming shrill.

"Mom," I said, "I think he was knocked unconscious by something or other. I think Pops is responsible, but we need not discuss anything except Uncle Paul's condition while we are at the hospital. We don't want to make any slips that could come back to haunt us later," I told them.

"Haunt us?" What do you mean haunt us?" my mother asked, annoyed. "I have nothing to hide!"

Before she could become more agitated, I cut in and answered, "Yes, Mom I know … this is my problem. I don't want anyone to associate me with him. I'm sorry, but I didn't pick him, remember? We'll leave in five minutes," I said abruptly, guilt washing over me because of my hurtful words to her.

To my surprise, they were waiting when I got there. After checking the house a second time, locking everything and wedging a chair under the front doorknob, I left through the side door. I knew he could come inside to greet us when we came home if he really wanted to. He would have no problem in doing so, but I indulged myself anyway. I had a pretty good idea where he might have gone … either he was lying on his canvas tarp bleeding, or he was in the loft peering through a hole in the wall, bleeding. Probably making plans for a comeback.

When we reached the end of the drive, I glanced toward the culvert. There was nothing in sight, and I turned off the drive and onto the road. We drove to the hospital and waited while the doctor examined Paul.

"He seems perfectly healthy except for a nasty bump on his head. We want to observe him overnight as a precaution; he can go home tomorrow," the doctor said.

"Thank you, doctor," I said, and my hand automatically touched the gun concealed in my belt. *This will give me time to take out the trash,* I thought. *Good! Yes, thank you, doctor, for keeping Uncle Paul while I do what I have to do.*

I called Patty and let her know that Paul had gotten a clean bill of health, and he would be home tomorrow. She sniveled a little. "Thank God!" she said.

"I'll tell him I talked to you, Patty, so now relax," I said. "I'm sure he will call you tomorrow."

I felt the gun tucked into my waist. *My God, how did I get here? How many lies are there between here and the fire that burns eternal?*

Once home, I pulled the car into the garage and procrastinated until my mother and Sharon had made their way out. I pulled the gun from my waist and checked it to see if it was loaded. It had four bullets left, with one in the chamber.

I closed the revolver, tucked it into my belt, and followed Mom and Sharon into the house. I wanted to conduct a search to see if there was anyone there who shouldn't be there.

I checked the house and didn't find anything suspicious, so I told Mom and Sharon to go into Mom's room and lock the door.

"Stay in your room until I tell you to come out," I told them.

"What are you going to do?" Mom asked.

"I'm going to find Pops and take care of this problem one way or another! This has gone far enough! If things get out of hand, I'll call the police," I reassured her. "This ends now!"

"I'm coming with you," she said, slipping the shoe she had just removed back on her foot.

"No, you aren't!" I argued.

"I said I'm coming with you," she said in her *this is the final word* voice.

"I'm coming, too!" Sharon chimed in. I looked at the two of them. Mom was defiant, Sharon was wide-eyed.

"So you know where he is, don't you?" Mom's voice rose.

"I don't know anything," I retorted. "You know as much as I."

"You have a hunch where he is. Don't you?" she persisted, her voice becoming agitated.

"Can't you just let it go?" I begged. "Can't you just let me check to see if I do know where he is? Would that be too difficult?" I whined, exasperated. "Why can't you do as I tell you, Mom? Is that too much to ask?"

"I'm glad you asked, dear; as a matter of fact, I could go and lock myself in my room and sit there like a simpleton until you tell me to come out, but no, I'm not willing to do that, so yes, I'm afraid it is asking too much," she said, exposing a side of her that I hadn't seen before.

"Here's what I think, Faye," Sharon said defiantly, coming to her mother's defense. "I think we should just call the police like normal people and then we could *all* lock ourselves in until they come. That's what I think."

The words "normal people" tripped a switch, turning on the consuming anger that had plagued me most of my life. "Normal people?" I asked, glaring at her. "Normal people? I'm not normal people! You're normal people, not me," I admonished her. "You're totally normal. Normal, normal you! You have no idea!" I fumed. "Lucky you!"

"It's not her fault, Faye," my mother interjected. "If you want to punish someone, punish me or keep your peace. You know what, Faye, I've changed my mind," she said, waving me off. "Do whatever you need to do, and we'll stay out of your way. Go fight your demons!"

I felt a thud in my chest as my heart hit bottom. "Okay," I said, "I will!" and I slammed the door behind me as I left.

Will this heart of mine, full of hatred and murder, eventually drive me to the gates of hell? I wondered. "I must be close," I whispered, touching the gun. "Very close." My resolve was evaporating. *How can I possibly do this?* I thought, *and besides that, I have no time! That's another obstacle.*

Franny appeared to me then, warning me … "If he's under the dirt ya have nothing to worry about. If he's not he runs his mouth and ya lose that fancy name of yers or maybe he kills a member of yer family. Figure it out, Phony. Will the real Faye Lawrence please stand up? Ha!" she snickered.

My phone rang. It was Kenneth. I was in no shape to talk to him until I pulled myself together, so I ignored it.

Damn it! I thought, my cheeks burning. *She has no reason to jump on me. If Sharon had ever had her ass beat she would understand,* I groused, *but she gets her mouth engaged when she knows absolutely nothing about life!*

My phone rang again. It was Kenneth. "Hi, killer," he said. For a moment I was shaken. *How does he know?* I thought.

"Oh Kenneth, it's so good to hear your voice," I said.

"Is everything all right, Faye?"

"Yes, why, do I sound desperate?"

"A little, I think."

"Well I'm not. How is Martin?" I asked

"He's standing here holding a note for me to read. It says you received a call at work from a Michael O'Leary who asked you to call him back. That's the message. Do you want his number?"

"Oh really? Interesting! Yes, I'll take it," I said

"That's not Crispy, is it?" he asked.

"No, it's the county prosecutor's office. Maybe I'll give him a call later. I applied for work there before I came to KADN."

There was a pause. "You did?" he asked. "Do you think you will take a job there?"

"I'm an attorney, you know, but I really haven't considered it yet. What's the number?" I asked. He gave me the number and I scratched it into the dust on my car. "Thanks … I do have some stories to tell you both, but not until we get together," I confided.

"Give me a hint," Kenneth begged.

"We'll talk later, my curious little friend. Greet Martin for me and remember you promised to keep your mouths shut," I said, sorry now that I had started the conversation about the stories I had for them.

"They have been shut. Really!" he said.

"I believe you."

"When are you coming home?" he asked.

"I'll be home soon," I answered. "I wish you were here with me."

"Me too. Has there been any sign of trouble there, Faye?" he asked. "I can't help but worry. I haven't been able to sleep thinking of him out there hunting you like this."

"Don't worry, Kenneth, I'll let you know if there's anything at all suspicious," I lied. "Crispy is probably half dead from having been burned and run over by the car! Don't worry, I'll be fine."

"Maybe it's me, but you sound so different. Is there anything I can do? Or … you haven't changed your mind about … you know … me calling you so much and everything, have you, Faye?" he asked.

"I wait for your calls, Kenneth, don't you know that? You know, I think I might be a little bored with life in the country. I'll be fine once I get home."

"Admit it! You miss me," he teased.

"All right, I do miss you," I said.

"Yeah?"

"Yeah!"

"You've made me very happy, firefly!" he laughed. "Now I can hang up. Say goodnight, love."

"Goodnight, love," I said and rang off. "Could you ever love me, Kenneth?" I whispered to myself. "Probably," I answered. I rehashed every word of our conversation, trying to hear some encrypted message that said, "I love you." I wanted that desperately, and I thought I heard it this time for sure. He had asked me if I had changed my mind about him calling me so often, as though it was very important to him. How else could you interpret that? "Oh well, forget it, it's silly I suppose!" I said.

I went into the garage and checked the revolver again to see if it was really ready to fire if I had to. Once I was sure of it, I turned the light off and stood in the dark, recalling my struggle to become the person I thought of as normal.

It all started so simply by wanting to be normal, and it had developed into a lifelong struggle to remake myself. To change myself into something I was not. *So now here I am standing in a darkened garage alone, still feeling alienated, still feeling separate.* I let my knees fold beneath me and slowly slipped to the floor. Tears stung my eyes. "Help me, God," I whispered. "Make me normal."

Chapter 28

This day was turning out to be one of self-examination and revelation. I resented Sharon for telling me how normal people conducted themselves because I was aware of my own covert and persistent feeling of being apart and not normal somehow. I asked myself if a normal person would plan to murder her own father, however true it was that he was scum from the depths of hell. On the one hand, it really burned me to hear what constituted "normal" from an innocent who never had a minute's worth of discomfort in her life—but on the other hand, who better to know about normal than one as normal as she?

I had raced through life hiding behind the illusion of accomplishment and respectability, all the while feeling inferior at my core. In my frenzied quest for equality, I had shut out those things that make life rich. It was finally clear to me now; I had lived an isolated life because I wanted to live a normal life filled with normal things, like respect, friendship, and love. It didn't make sense.

"Enough! Is that your answer, Lord? Are you going to help me or not?" I fumed. "I must get out of this damned dark garage; maybe it will be a little less depressing," I said aloud.

My heart stopped for a moment when I opened the door and there in the sunlight stood Pops. He hadn't noticed me; he was watching the house intently. He reminded me of a Springer spaniel pointing out his quarry. I quietly shrunk back and eased the door closed, but I didn't latch it for fear he would hear the mechanism. I went to the window where I could watch him from the dimly lighted garage without him knowing. The question was, how many times had Pops stood here in the darkened garage, watching? I looked at the floor to see if there were any flat cigarette butts. There were!

I could see that he had a knife tucked into his belt, and he carried something that looked like a rock the size of a baseball. He must have picked up a rock from the edge of a small flower garden that Patty had made, lined on the perimeter with small rocks to block grass from invading it. God only knows what he planned to do with that … I didn't want to imagine, but I couldn't help deducing that maybe he was going to break the window with it, so he could surprise those inside.

That was the first time I had really gotten a good look at him since I lit him on fire in the car. I could definitely see where his hair and brows were burned away and fuzzy looking. His face was red and blotchy too, where the flames had singed him, but he definitely was able to see, and right now he was intent on watching something inside the house. He moved himself this way and that to gain a better perspective of something that was completely obstructed from my view by a small deck that protruded out from the house.

"What are you looking for, you nasty old pedophile?" I whispered. "Are you lonely? Don't worry, scum from hell, you aren't going to be lonely for long."

I touched my revolver as I watched him, and I tried to imagine which scenario would occupy his worst nightmare. A bullet to his temple would certainly be high on his list, but a long lonely stretch in jail, where he had no control over anyone, not even himself—that trumps a bullet. *Those are the footsteps he hears behind him in the dark,* I thought. *That's his nightmare!*

I watched him for a time, and then I dialed the police, barely able to see the dial because of tears I shed for some unknown reason. Probably because calling the police was the first step on a long journey. It was normal. It would certainly blow my cover. I wondered how the name Franny would feel. Not good at all, I concluded.

"We've had an intruder," I told them. "We shot at him earlier and I think we may have wounded him. There were traces of blood. Unfortunately, he has returned, and he is here now peeping in our window. Please hurry!" I urged. "We know who this man is. He's dangerous, we're afraid of him."

I couldn't leave my post, so I called Mom and Sharon and told them that Pops was standing just outside the house, and that they should lock the door and stay put. "I know, Faye, we already called the police," Mom confessed.

"Good! I called them too," I said quietly. "I'll stay here and watch him until the police get here."

"Did you lock the door out there? What if he comes in there?" Mom asked.

"I'm afraid he would hear me lock it," I whispered. "I don't want him to leave until they get here. I have your gun with me, so I'm fine. I'll stay put. By the way, can he see you from where he is or what?"

"I've been making a trip by the window every now and then so he won't know we see him," she answered.

"Tell Sharon I'm sorry that I snapped at her," I said.

"Ha!" she snorted. "Tell her yourself, after the police haul him away."

"All right, I will," I smiled. "Mom, where did you get this gun?" I asked.

"Ernie," she answered, "a long time ago."

I watched while he poked around by the window that seemed to intrigue him. I was sure he must have been waiting for a glimpse of Sharon. He probably thought Uncle Paul was at home, or he would have broken the door in and kidnapped her as he had threatened to do. Another possibility was that he waited for me to be present so that he could have an opportunity to take revenge on both of us and especially me for burning him.

I kept watching him as time dragged on at an almost unbearably slow pace. Once before I had wondered how he had become the dangerous criminal that he was. Now, watching him standing alone, wounded and disheveled, peeking through the window at the life he could have had, I wondered what monster had impacted his life and sent him down his road of personal destruction. How he had arrived at this point in his life would probably always be a mystery, but still I was curious.

For a moment, I pictured him as a little boy, lonely and beaten, peeking through the window, watching a loving family within and wishing … wishing to be normal.

I felt a tug at my heart. I felt the hatred I held for him melt away, and I was left with nothing but pity for him. *I have forgiven him!* I thought.

I blessed myself. "Am I finally free, Lord?" I asked.

"Are you?" The answer came back as a question. "It's up to you, isn't it?"

I watched two police cars pull slowly up the long drive-way between the white board fences and slowly stop once they came to the place where the drive swings around and turns back on itself to form a large turn-about by the front door of the old house.

Two of the officers got out of the first patrol car and start-ed toward the front door.

I looked for Pops, and he was gone! My attention had been diverted while I watched the police approach, and I had let him slip away.

I looked around in a panic at each nook and cranny that could offer him a place to hide. Then I spotted him crouched behind a shrub by the corner of the house.

Obviously he was too weakened from his wounds to make a mad dash for freedom, and so he squatted behind a bush, a frightened child with his knife tucked in his belt.

"Hello," I called from the garage door. "I think you are looking for the man over there under the shrub," I said, pointing at Pops.

He didn't make an attempt to escape but rose to a stand-ing position. The officers ordered, "Go to the ground, hands out to the side."

Pops answered with a flurry of obscenities befitting a man losing his freedom, and he didn't go to the ground. Instead, he stood defenseless and defiant, slinging accusations at the police and the dirty bitches that called them.

"He has a knife in his belt," I called.

"Drop the knife," the officer ordered.

"Yer not tellin' me what ta do, so shut yer Goddamned mouth!" Pops yelled.

"Drop the knife and go to the ground, I told you!" the officer demanded.

"Ya better git yer ass back up the road where ya come from if ya don't wan'to git yerselves a ass kickin', ya bastards," Pops threatened.

"I will have to control you in one way or another, so how do you want this to end?" the officer asked, holding his revolver in both hands straight out in front of himself.

"Yer gunna have ta kill me cause I'm not gun-na go back till those two bitches … are …" Pops voice trailed off as he lost consciousness, went to his knees, and then fell face first to the ground.

The two cops rushed forward with the others following close behind. They handcuffed Pops and flipped him over, removing the large knife in his belt that he had taken from the kitchen.

"He's bleeding; my God, he's been shot!" the officer said. "Call Rescue, Eddie, I think he's in a bad way."

"Christ All-mighty," Eddie said. "This is that goddamned con everybody's been lookin' for! Hey, we caught an escaped convict. Whoa! He looks like he's been over a hundred miles of bad road! Ha!"

"Keep a civil tongue in your mouth; you're an officer of the law, not a stinking comedian!" the older of the two scolded. "I'm not kidding this time, call Rescue, do it now!"

I joined Mother and Sharon on the porch and waited for the police to finish their business with Pops. The two of them left Pops and joined the three of us on the porch.

"Hello, I'm Frank Walters. Were you the ones who reported the break-in?" he asked.

"Yes we are … the break-in and the shooting," Mom declared, turning defiantly to me as she spoke.

"Are you aware that this man is a wanted escapee from the state prison?" he asked.

"Oh yes, we certainly are; we know all about him," Mom asserted. "We couldn't be more aware of who he is!"

"We'll take him out of here as soon as the medics come. We'll get him patched up, and he'll be on his way."

"What a relief that will be," Mom said. "Thank you! Make sure you keep him in there this time!"

Chapter 29

"Kenneth, what time is it?" I asked.

"Let me see … it's exactly one thirty-one PM," he answered.

"Well, I have a hot scoop for you. It's about the escaped convict. Are you interested?" I teased.

"Duh … let me see … yes! Spill it, firefly," he said.

"Well then, here it is: Nick Beck was captured at one-twelve PM this afternoon by the Fenwick Police. He didn't resist and went quietly. Well … sort of! I have all the details so you can go with it right away!" I gushed.

"In Fenwick proper?" he asked.

"Ah … well … no, they caught him … here but not in the …"

"Hold on, where is 'here,' Faye?"

"At my uncle's place … I guess." Suddenly, I realized that I had made a huge mistake by keeping him in the dark about everything, and that he wasn't going to receive this as it was intended.

"Are you telling me that the escaped convict was caught at your home?" he asked, astonished.

"I guess," I answered.

"So Faye, I'm … *guessing* … the 'crispy critter' and the escaped convict are, after all, one and the same person. Is that too close to the truth for you?"

I could hear in his voice that he was irritated. It had been a huge mistake to keep him at arm's length throughout this ordeal. I felt contrite and guilty. I had promised to keep him involved in everything but had, instead, secreted information away from him. I remembered his calls each day, telling me exactly what was happening in his life. It was a trust issue now. Deceit simply didn't suit his personality; he was fuming inside. The truth was that I did it to shelter him, but that sounded trite now, a weak excuse. I remained silent.

"Faye, do you hear me?"

"Yes, I do," I answered.

"Are you going to tell me that the escaped convict is the critter?" he asked again.

"Well anyway," I interjected. "I'm driving home tomorrow evening, and I want to meet you and Martin at the Moon. I can tell you everything then. Can you be there?"

"Faye, just give me the fucking truth for a change. Is that convict and Crispy Critter the same person? Yes or no! Say it!" he demanded.

"I guess," I admitted.

"You *guess* he is?" I could hear impatience building in his voice, and I was starting to get very nervous. "Is he the same person as the critter? Yes or no!"

"I guess," I answered softly.

"You're *guessing* again?" he snapped. "Oh my God! … Don't say 'I guess' again or I'll have a fucking stroke. Simply tell the truth … are you capable of that, Faye?"

"He is."

"Blessed Father … how did the police catch him?" he quizzed.

"Can we talk about it tomorrow?" I asked.

"Now, Faye!" he demanded.

"We called them," I answered.

"So you spotted him today and called the police? Where was he when you spotted him?"

"No … Well … Okay, I did get a letter from him a few days ago, and it was posted in Fenwick, so we knew he was either coming here or was already here, but he didn't do anything until today."

"You … got a letter a few days ago? Why is he writing to you? We talked so many times since then, and you lied to me over and over again. You said things to me … things that I … well, never mind … I'll never believe it again. Not from you!"

"Kenneth, please, I meant everything! Everything I told you about us."

"Riiight! Well, anyway, may I ask you what you mean by 'do anything'?"

"Well, okay. I'll give you the whole sequence. He wrote a threatening letter saying he was coming here. He came here today … Today! He knocked my uncle unconscious and broke in. He tried to abduct my little sister because he knew that would kill my mother. Mom shot him in self-defense.

He left but came back later. We called the police. They came and arrested him. That's it," I said.

"Shot him?" He was incredulous.

"That's right, she shot him," I answered, feeling a little angry now.

"So everyone is safe now?" he asked.

"Yes, we're all safe now, Kenneth," I answered.

"Nice!" he said coldly, and the phone went silent.

After a few moments I asked, "Kenneth ... Kenneth are you there?"

"So Faye, let me get this straight," he said icily. "We talked after you got the letter, right?"

"Yes."

"After he knocked your uncle out, am I right?"

"Right."

"We talked ... after he tried to kidnap your sister ... that's right too, isn't it?"

"Yes, I'm sorry."

"Your mother shot him, and we talked after that, correct? We talked after all those things, and you still didn't say a damned word to me. You promised to keep me on the inside. I thought you ... never mind ... what am I to you, the joke of the day? Does it turn your crank to hurt someone who ... cares for you? What the hell's wrong with you, Faye?"

"Kenneth, I'm sorry, truly sorry," I said. "I didn't want to worry you, and those last three things did happen simultaneously."

"Oh, well ... now I feel warm and fuzzy all over since I know three things happened simultaneously, but still, you kept all three of them, and more, a secret from me!"

"I guess."

"Yes, well ... and I bet you 'guessed' it was none of my damned business anyway, right? Nice! Forgive me, Faye, I thought we were ... were something ... that we're not!" he said. "You put me on the outside! You lied to me! Fine! I get it!"

"I'm sorry, Kenneth," I said.

"Yes, I am too!" he answered. "Anyway, you said you would like to have lunch with Martin and me when you get in. Well, I hate to tell you this: Martin has gone back with his wife, so I can't speak for him, and as for me, I'll have to check my calendar. Soooo ... I'll let you know," he finished.

"Don't, please, Kenneth," I pleaded. "I'm truly sorry! You're really important to me."

"I wonder how the shoe would feel on your foot? So I just have to ask you. What am I to you?" he asked.

"More than you could know. I think of you all of the time," I whispered.

"Is there anything you say that isn't a fucking lie, Faye? Anything at all that you can think of that isn't a lie? Nothing in the world galls me more than dishonesty! Nothing I despise more than ... a damned liar!"

"Oh please, Kenneth, I want to tell you," I wept openly. "I need to tell you ... who I am. I have a horrible secret."

There was a long silence; I was uncomfortable, fearing that he would hang up and walk out of my life forever.

"Yeah?" he finally asked softly. We both fell silent for a moment.

"Yeah," I whispered. "I can be there by eight-thirty in the evening tomorrow for sure. Will you be there?" I asked.

"Maybe," he answered. "I don't know. Maybe you could drive home tonight, Faye. Why not just get this over with, one way or another?"

"My Uncle Paul is in the hospital because of his head injury, and we expect him home tomorrow, so I want to make sure he's all right before I leave. Will you meet me tomorrow?" I asked.

"I'll see. I told you, I'm not sure about Martin, he's been running circles around himself trying to make things work with his wife."

"Well, that's all right then. Isn't it?" I asked. "I mean … the two of us?"

"I don't know, Faye. What could you tell me that will put it together again? What could you say that I would … believe? I haven't slept in days," he said. "I need some rest. Maybe now that he's in jail … if he is in jail … I can get some sleep tonight. I'll think on it, maybe things will look better in the morning."

"I'll be home tomorrow, Kenneth," I said. "I'll be at the Moon at eight-thirty."

"Have a safe trip, Faye," he said.

"I will, thank you," I said. I needed to hear him tell me to "say goodnight, love," the way he always had, but the phone went dead. I was afraid it was the end for us, and I was heartsick. I hung up and started gathering my things, eager for the drive home the next day. *I can't wait; will I be able to fix things, or will you run away now because I've deceived you, Kenneth?*

The dice were cast; they had already skittered into the backboard and turned … SNAKE EYES! … I lose!

"Please … let me roll 'em again?"

Part Five

Chapter 30

Uncle Paul arrived home early in the morning in perfect health, driving a rented car and needing no one's help. He called Patty first thing and told her that he was "fit as a fiddle." When he hung up, after an incredibly long time, he listened incredulously to our story about Nick's apprehension.

He had no memory of the events that led to his being knocked unconscious by the old convict, and we had no idea what happened either. When we had finished telling him the story, he called Patty back and filled her in. They were a joyful couple, and their history went back to their high school days, when the Lawrence family first migrated to America from England and settled in North Dakota becoming ranchers. Their relationship was easy and confident.

"I'm lucky Nick loves me," he told Patty, "or he might have snubbed me altogether. Ha!" The English have a certain charm about them, I thought. A soft edge if you will.

I threw my things into my smelly car as soon as I could make a graceful exit and started home. I drove straight through as darkness was falling, my eyes squinting against the setting sun. The journey seemed to take forever, but finally I arrived at the Moon Café.

Kenneth's Mercedes was parked in front in plain view. My heart raced when I saw it. He had gotten out of his car and was standing beside it, watching me as I walked up. When I saw him, I felt tearful. He pulled me to himself and held my head against his chest gently with his hands; his scent was all around me. Tears began to flow. "I'm sorry, Kenneth," I said. "I really am."

"Please don't apologize, we'll talk it out. It'll be all right. I should not have reacted as I did … It was a stressful experience … I'm sorry if I hurt you in any way. We'll have a nice dinner, and then we'll talk," he said, but he didn't smile when our eyes met. Instead, he offered me his arm and not his lips and led me into the Moon Café. I felt ill. Our roles had completely switched. I had always been the dominant party in our friendship, but in love he was definitely the force, and I was the acquiescent participant. How did I let this happen?

"For two," he told the hostess, "a private booth please, so we can talk."

"Okay, Ken," she said and led us to the corner booth where we had sat so many times before with Martin.

"How are you two this evening?" she asked.

"Peachy!" Kenneth answered dismissively. "Send us a bottle of your house wine, and give us a few minutes before you send our waitress. We want to catch up a bit." As soon as we had settled in, he smiled across the table and offered me his hand palm up. I put my hand in his and dropped my eyes. I felt my face flush a little.

"Look at me, Faye," he said. "No tears, let's just enjoy whatever time we have together. We'll have our dinner, and then you can tell me whatever it is you want me to hear. I promise I'll listen with my heart, I really will, and then we'll see where we go from there ... fair enough?"

"Yes ... I understand," I said.

We ordered and sat talking about work-related subjects that occurred after I had taken my vacation and other light-hearted small talk. The way we had when we first met, like casual acquaintances. We finished our dinner and sat sipping our wine. The conversation fell silent with the expectation that we would talk about the gaping fissure that was separating us. I finally surrendered to the inevitable conclusion that I must tell him my secrets as I had promised if I hoped to hold him, and in return I hoped that he would share the burden of knowing them ... that he would not run.

"This is really hard for me, Kenneth," I told him, "because I can see that your feelings for me have changed, and I'm still stuck with the same old feelings I always had for you. I don't think that will ever change," I said. "I've never had anything like we had before; I mean, you were sort of like my ... lover, I mean boyfriend or something. You kissed me like ... you know ... lovers, I guess. Oh my God ... I wanted you to think I was special and good so much! Ha! That's the biggest lie of all; I'm neither special nor good," I told him. I couldn't look at him, so I looked into my wine glass. This was even harder than I had anticipated.

Kenneth got up and came around to my side of the booth and took my hand. I didn't look at him, and I pulled my hand away and shaded my eyes with it. I continued talking into my wine glass.

"You want to know if I lied to you. My whole life is a lie, but I promise I won't lie to you anymore. All I want is for you to trust me again someday. This is the first time I've ever told anyone about myself. The only thing I ask is that you keep my secret and that you don't judge me; I didn't want this life, I've been hiding from it. Anyway, I was the oldest in a really dysfunctional family. Our last name was Beck."

"What? Wait a minute ... your family name was Beck and now it's Lawrence?" Kenneth asked.

"No," I said. "I've never been married, if that's what you're thinking, okay. Look, I'm not going to beat around the bush, Kenneth, I'll clear it up right now. Nick Beck is my father ... mystery solved!"

"Stop it! My God! Faye, stop it ... now. It's all coming together ... are you telling me that Nick Beck, the escaped convict, who is the same person as the crispy critter, is also your father?"

"I'm afraid so, Kenneth. I'm telling you up front, Nick Beck is my father. I should have told you a long time ago," I said. "Maybe things could have worked out differently between us."

"Honey, I'm sorry, I really am ... I'm just ... I can't get my mind around this," he said. "Your father is the convict who tried to kill you?"

"Ha! I wish that were all, Kenneth, my life today as you know it, it's all a story that I made up. You have no idea what my life has been, and you have no idea how sick I am of all of it! The mask is coming off, Kenneth; I'm tired of lying, and I'm sick of being alone. I don't want to drone on about it endlessly," I said, "but I brought it on myself by pretending to be someone I wasn't. The truth is, I'm tired of the whole goddamned fight."

"Blessed Father," Kenneth said to neutralize my blasphemy.

"Hey, if you want to leave because of something I tell you ... you'll just have to go for it! If you want to hear the rest of my weird story, I'll tell you. If you have any questions when I'm finished, ask me, I'll tell you the truth."

"I just want to hear whatever you want me to know, that was our agreement. I don't want to hear one syllable about anything you don't want me to know. If you're having second thoughts about it, don't tell me anything. I have to tell you, though; I am getting a little uncomfortable with this whole arrangement," Kenneth said. "I wasn't prepared to have you tell me things that you would rather I didn't know."

"I know I've told you a lot of fairy-tale crap about myself," I ignored him and continued. "Now I want you to meet the real me. I have two brothers, Willard and Charles, and then there's Sharon, my sister, fourteen years younger than I. She's the youngest one in my family, the only one who lived a normal life. If you want to know the truth, I resent her for that to this very day, because it should have been my life as well! Our family home was a hovel; it was hidden in the woods, in a valley, miles away from the nearest human being. The place was a pit, and we lived like animals."

Once I started to tell him who I was, I told it all, all of the soul-crushing details. It was as if the dam had burst, and everything flowed out. All of the rotten facts came crashing forward and I didn't spare him anything. To hell with his sensitivities; he wants the truth, and I can deliver it!

At times, Kenneth would cover his face with his hands and shake his head slowly as he listened. Something deep inside me took pleasure in that. *You wanted it, Mr. never-had-your-ass-beat! Well, here it is!*

Finally, I thought I had said enough. It was probably too much. It had taken a huge leap of faith on my part. Nothing was cleaned up or altered. I told him about the molestation, the boxcar, the Christmas program, my monster, the whip, my rage, how I had changed my name, and even about Franny's appearances.

Finally, frustrated, I gave it up; with all that talking, I hadn't gotten to the core of the problem. I hadn't told him the real story. I was unable to articulate to him what had really happened to me, because it wasn't the individual events. Each one of them was probably survivable by itself, but collectively they had altered me. That's what I wanted to tell him. The abuse had proven to me over and over again that I was a nonperson, someone without value, nothing more than a utility, a receptacle for sexual debris, and a punching bag to be used when the release of emotional stress was needed ... was desired!

It was because the humiliation and dehumanizing sexual abuse was a daily occurrence from before I had memory until I was fourteen years old. It was all the days in a year, multiplied by all those years, which had written an indelible message on my psyche. *It was your fault ... you're dirty ... no one loves you ... stay out of sight ... don't tell anyone ... you caused it ... don't trust anyone ... hide yourself.*

I wanted him to understand that, when I was finally freed from that abuse, I had no choice other than to stand before the mirror and say, "Hello, my name is Faye ... Faye Lawrence." I had to lie to myself ... because it made me believe that I had found a sliver of light shining through a crack somewhere in fate's armor, a ray of hope ... that I had found anonymity.

I felt resentment and anger rise within me now. *Sorry I fibbed, you self-centered prick!* I thought.

"I'm tired," I told him. "I'll save the rest for later, if you ever want to hear it." I was inflamed with resentment. "Oh, one more thing, my name is legally Faye Lawrence, and that's what I prefer to be called."

"You know you'll never hear anything different from me, Faye," he answered, looking bewildered, and then angry. "Why in hell did you say that to me?"

"I don't know, I'm just frustrated." *It's not his fault,* I thought. "I trust you, Kenneth, and I want you to know, I never intended to shut you out. I wanted to shelter you from finding out about me," I said. My resentment was subsiding a little now. It wasn't his fault.

"I know, honey, I know," he said. "I'm ready to get out of here, are you?"

"Yes, I'm ready," I told him.

"Would you walk with me?" he asked. He settled the bill and said goodnight to our waitress, and we left the Moon. We walked along the tree-lined walkway in silence. Kenneth had pulled his coat back and had both hands in his pant pockets. He often did that.

He walked slowly, looking down at the walkway, deep in thought. I wondered what he was thinking. I was apprehensive as we walked along together and still a little angry for some reason.

He shook his head now and then; I thought he might be having second thoughts about any kind of a relationship with me. *Or maybe he thinks I'm a phony, and what have you to offer me in return for my confession?* I thought. *Are you going to turn up the heat a little? To hell with that!*

"You do realize you need to work with a therapist, don't you?" he asked without looking at me.

"Well, I don't know. Am I that bad?" I asked. "I've been doing better lately."

He stopped and turned to me, looking at me intently, with his hands still in his pockets. "You have some serious issues, Faye. The voices and the rage, that's serious stuff! And that Franny business, that's bizarre. I think your problems should have been addressed a long time ago. You were an innocent little girl … and no one helped you; it breaks my heart to say this, but you have to get some help. I mean professional help, Faye," he finished.

"Yes, you're right, Kenneth, I should go to a stranger and get some help," I smiled. "I'll just tell them my story and they'll give me a magic pill that'll make it all better … and no one will ever have to be bothered with me or my problems again. Sound good?"

"Stop it! Stop it right now! That's bullshit, and you know it! Don't tag me with that! I'm not a weasel—when I want to get rid of you, I'll let you know!" he stormed. "I'm seeing a different side of you, Faye. I think you need help with your problems, help that I'm not qualified to give you. Is that offensive for some reason?"

"Kenneth," I said, "I'm afraid I've lost you. You called me a liar, so I wanted to give you the truth, but now I feel like you've lost respect for me. I feel so … like you don't understand. I need what we had before. You've changed toward me, and I'm so … lonely!"

"Lonely for me?" he asked. "I'm right here. Nothing has changed for me, Faye … you too?" he asked.

I came over to him then. "Nothing has changed for you then?" I asked.

"Well, I won't lie, I may have flown a little too close to the flame, I may have sustained a little singe I guess, but no, I still … care. Nothing has changed that way; I still care for you, Faye."

When I fell in love with Kenneth, it wasn't a sexual attraction right away. I had fallen in love with him from my heart and head because I loved who he was, how he conducted himself, and truthfully the way he looked as well. It was after I fell in love with him that all of the trappings revealed themselves to me, and now there were so many of them. I had developed a sexual obsession for him almost, but in my defense, I had loved his heart before I lusted for his mouth.

I had learned early in my life that the only commodity I had to trade was giving sexual gratification. Maybe my need to mend things with Kenneth was the driving force behind my obsession. Who knows, maybe I was trying to trade sex for love.

He took my hand in his and, pulling his coat back, put his hand in his pocket with mine inside his, squeezing it in a gentle caress. We walked along like that, in silence. I could feel his thigh moving against my hand as he walked. I smelled his scent and caught my breath as a thrill ripped through my body in response to his touch.

"C'mon, Faye," he said, his voice husky. "Let's go home."

We walked hand in hand back to the Moon Café, my head on his shoulder like a couple in love. I loved him, and I wanted to give myself to him completely, body and soul. This was a new beginning for me. The first time my body had ever yearned for a lover. *Oh Kenneth, it had to be you,* I thought, *it could only be you.* When we reached the Moon, instead of Kenneth taking me to his Mercedes, carrying me off to his lair, and covering my mouth with his, he led me to my car.

"I'll follow you home," he said and opened the door to my car. I slid in dumbfounded and embarrassed. I had thrown myself at him, and he was refusing me. I felt like I had been slapped! I should have known better! Who could love me?

I had flung the dice again; they had scampered away and slammed into the backboard; SNAKE EYES! I lost again!

I just want to go home! I thought, and I slammed the door shut and started the motor.

"I'll be right behind you," he said, bending down to talk into my window.

"Don't worry about me, I can find my own way home," I snapped and drove off, leaving him bending in the street where he was standing. I was furious that he had stuffed me into my car without so much as a "May I kiss you good-night?" *There is no reason for me to be alive,* I thought. *Why did I do this? Stupid fool!* I drove my car into the garage and closed the door. I took the stairs two at a time up to my apartment. I rammed the key into the lock and went in, slamming the door behind me. I felt the fire of blind rage gathering in my chest.

"Goddamn it!" I cursed. "Why? Now he thinks I'm a fucking whore. God! He made me think he loved me," I sobbed, slipping to the floor.

My phone rang. I looked. It said Kenneth. I don't even want to talk to that fucking idiot, I thought. How dare he call me!

I decided to answer it. *He's never going to know how much he hurt me. At least I can try to salvage some of my pride.*

"Hi, Kenneth, what's up?" I answered casually.

"Where did you go, honey?"

"Where did I go?"

"Faye, I'm waiting out here. How long does it take you to park a car?"

"Oh … well … well, I had to run up for a minute."

"Will you be much longer?" he asked. "I can come up and wait if you're going to be a while."

"No, I'll just be a minute," I said. I hung up and dashed into the bathroom to repair my face, and then I ran down the stairs and into his waiting car.

"Sorry," I said.

"No problem, honey," he said, holding his hand out, palm up waiting for mine. *I definitely do need a therapist,* I thought. *Kenneth is right about that!*

Kenneth pulled into his parking place and came around. I waited for him. He opened my door and offered me his hand. I took it and he helped me out; reaching back in for my jacket, he slipped it on my shoulders.

I wondered if anyone had the right to feel such joy. We walked to his apartment. He had his hand on the small of my back, guiding me as he walked with me. I felt as though I belonged to him. I was giddy with love. Once inside, he hung my jacket up. "Make yourself comfortable, Faye. I'll grab a couple of glasses and some wine and be right there. You like white, right?"

"Thanks, I do prefer white."

Kenneth poured two glasses of wine, passed one to me, and raised the other in a toast. "To us?" he asked.

"To us," I answered.

He patted the seat beside himself, inviting me to sit by him. I got up and came over to him. Once there, he put his arms around me and gave me his mouth, gently.

"Faye, may I bore you with something I think you should know about me? Don't worry, it's the short version ... I promise."

"I'm not going to be shocked, am I? You know I have tender sensitivities, don't you?" I teased.

"That's what attracted me to you," he said. "Well ... that and that wonderful pinch, you know, the one with the nifty twisting finish."

"You're asking for another one. You've had fair warning!" I told him.

"So anyway, Faye, let me tell you something, before I change my mind. You know my life has been the polar opposite of yours. My parents coddled my brother and me shamelessly."

"I can understand that, Kenneth," I said.

"Shhhh, I think this is something you should hear. I was just a normal kid, lots of friends, you know. I played sports, baseball mostly, but other sports as well. I graduated from the University of St. Thomas with a degree in business, and after that I spent four years in seminary."

"Seminary?"

"Right." he said. "Seminary. I studied to become a priest, but when it was time to take my vows, I couldn't bring myself to take them. You've heard that the spirit is strong but the flesh is weak? I wish that weren't the case, but that's me. I didn't have confidence, you know, that I could honor my vows to be celibate among other things, so I couldn't make the promise. I just have to be positive I can honor the vows. It really sent me over the edge for a while, Faye, but I'm learning to live with it. I guess I'm still reeling. I don't know why it happened. It happened, that's all … it just happened. Long story short, that's why you found me in a flunky job at dear old KADN television station … I'm sulking!"

"Kenneth, you could be a deacon in the church, couldn't you?"

"I don't think so, Faye; that seems like half of a cup to me. I want to drink the whole cup or nothing at all. I had a calling, and I refused it. I either go back all the way or jump ship altogether. I mean, I can't have it both ways. When I take my vows, I have to give myself, you know, the whole thing, without reservation. I can't pick and choose which parts of the vow I want to honor."

"I understand," I said. I knew that left me out … I was outside with my nose against the window again. I wanted in.

Kenneth put his arms around me and pressed his mouth over mine in a long, gentle, probing kiss. My body tensed to his touch. He gasped when I ran my hand down his smooth shirt and under his belt. I could feel his body react.

"Faye!" he said hoarsely, grabbing my arm to stop me. "Stop it ... stop it! Please! We can't."

I was hurt by his rejection. "Why don't you want me, Kenneth?"

"Why don't I want you? I'm trying to control myself here, Faye. I want us, and especially you, to work with a therapist first, so if we do come together we'll be whole and healthy, and I just told you, I have problems that I have to resolve. We have to figure out where we are here. You tell me, honey, would you want to let me have you right now? Even with everything I've told you?" he asked. "Are you sexually active now, Faye?"

"You don't trust me, do you? You still think I'm a liar. Don't you? I've never even shared a kiss before you. How could you ask me that? You think I'm a sex addict? I was raped when I was little, I didn't choose it. You think I'm sexual trash?" I protested angrily, my cheeks pulsating.

"I didn't mean to imply that you were lying or that you had a sexual addiction. I owe you a big apology; it isn't that I didn't believe what you told me. It's because I was looking for an excuse ... to think it wouldn't be as bad if ... if it were to happen, you know, between us. I feel like a louse! Please forgive me, Faye."

"We should see the therapist," I admitted. *I'll be damned if I'll let you off the hook that easy,* I thought.

"Do you forgive me? Please!"

"I guess it doesn't matter anyway," I sulked. "You're going to be a priest, so what's the point? We wait, we don't wait. What's the difference, Kenneth?"

"Faye, please tell me you forgive me. I need you to forgive me!"

"You become a priest and that excludes me from your future, you don't become a priest and you're miserable. Kenneth, you're not available!" I still wanted to punish him, so I withheld forgiveness from him.

"Why do you think I took pains to tell you about it?" he asked.

"You said you would be with me if I made myself healthy; you can't promise that, because either way we're doomed," I answered.

"Faye, I didn't tell you I would be with you forever, and I'm not saying I won't, because I don't know. I have problems to work through. I'm not trying to deceive you, honey. I think I'm … in love with you."

Those words that I had waited for were finally spoken, they were mine to remember for a lifetime. "I love you too, Kenneth," I said. "I really do, and you know I forgive you. Don't you?"

"Yeah?" he asked.

"Yeah," I answered him.

Chapter 31

Suddenly, the world revolved around Kenneth and me. It seemed that the sun rose for us alone and set so that we could have long magical evenings together. We made sure that at the end of those evenings, I slept alone and Kenneth did also. We began to work with a therapist. Sometimes together, but most times she would separate us and talk to each one of us individually.

The more I understood the effect my childhood had on my emotional health, the more happiness seeped into my life. Fewer and fewer self-recriminations invaded my thinking. I accepted the truth finally. I was Franny, Franny was me, and I was the victim of unspeakable abuse over which I had no control. Sounds so simple, right? No! Wrong!

There was much to forgive myself for before I could find serenity. Memories of tattling on Willie, Chuck, or my mother to ingratiate myself with my abuser—so that he would go easy on me—haunted me. There were so many memories that seemed to lie in wait and then storm in suddenly and take control.

The road to recovery was slow and strewn with pitfalls. Guilt and self-loathing were hard habits to break, but little by little I was able to embrace the powerless child who had failed to be honorable sometimes, a child who had sometimes been a co-conspirator with the evil old abuser. Once I understood that she had no choice, I began to forgive her and took her into my heart.

Kenneth and I had no secrets from each other. He had nothing to fear from complete honesty. I, on the other hand, was faced with a huge leap of faith to do the same. Nonetheless, I gave him all of my sins and secrets to do with as he would. Maybe he was to be mine, and I knew I was already his.

I wanted nothing more in the world than to lie in a marriage bed with him and to spend the rest of our lives locked in that promise. I was always sexually stimulated, and the obsession was a guilty pleasure. Just saying his name made an inferno of desire flame up in my belly. It was almost pleasurable when it happened, but it left me wanting more; it tormented me night and day.

We didn't advertise our relationship; we kept it from the people we worked with, except for Martin. He was our confederate in everything.

We would meet at the Moon as we always had. Martin wasn't always there, but he was there sometimes, still giddy from his reunion with his wife.

Kenneth told me, "I'm afraid that relationship is doomed from the onset. I hope I'm wrong," he would say. "Martin is so invested in it."

I thought secretly that they had a better chance at success than Kenneth and I, but I held my tongue.

By the time Kenneth and I finished our first set of sessions with our therapist, it was springtime. Water ran everywhere as the snow gave way to the warmth of spring.

It was a happy time of rebirth in nature, but for Kenneth and me the temptation to succumb to a sexual encounter was always there. It was taking its toll on our relationship.

There were times when we had long sessions of heavy petting—panting, gasping, and writhing in our lust for one another. We were more eager than ever to share our bodies, and our frustration surfaced in many different ways. Sometimes we had meaningless spats, and sometimes we shed tears of frustration. I was afraid that we were drifting apart. The elephant was always in the room. How many times can you say "I will resist" before desire dies? One cannot sustain extreme heightened sexual tension forever. Something has to give.

"I should wait for some fucking therapist to give me permission?" I stormed at Kenneth. "She probably wants you for herself!"

"Honey, do you hear yourself?" Kenneth asked.

"I'm just … Sorry," I answered.

"Can you wait just a little longer?" he asked.

"I'm trying," I said.

"Give me your hand, honey."

"Why?" I asked, putting my hand out.

"Give me the other one," he said.

"Well, why? Don't you dare slap my knuckles," I laughed, putting my left hand behind me.

"Just give it to me, okay?" he coaxed.

"Oh my God," I whispered, "my left?"

"Blessed Father … Left would be good, yeah?" he asked.

"Yeah, left is very good!" I whispered.

Kenneth knelt before me and slipped his ring on my finger. "Will you be Mrs. Kenneth Murphy?" he asked, looking almost shy, his eyes full of love.

"Oh, Kenneth, you know I will," I whispered.

He remained on his knees and pulled me to himself, his arms wrapped around my hips and his face turned into my waist. "I'm yours," he said, turning his face up to me. "I've given you my ring, and you're mine, right?" he asked.

"Always … you know I am," I answered.

He stood and took my hand and led me into the bedroom, closing the door behind us to shut out the rest of the world.

"This is our time," he told me, pulling his shirt over his head and stepping out of his clothes. That was the first time I saw him naked, saw his muscular thighs and his flat belly. He inflamed me with desire; I watched him slip onto the bed, knees first. He held his arm out to me, beckoning to me with his hand. "C'mere."

"I am, Kenneth," I whispered, barely able to speak, my body frozen with anticipation.

"You am?" he whispered into my hair, mocking me.

"Yeah," I whimpered, wrapping my arm around him. "I want you."

Our wait was over. Nothing existed except him, his body, his hard thighs, his soft lips, his scent all around me; I had them, and they were mine. My obsession for him had finally come to fruition, and the rest of the world just didn't matter; my lover had shut the door, locking it out!

I flung them, and they came up sevens! Yes!

Kenneth and I didn't leave our bed for the rest of the evening. We didn't rise to eat or bathe but took our fill of each other until sleep finally crept up quietly and stole what remained of our special night. In the morning, I woke and reached for him, but the bed was cold where he had slept. He was already up and had left the bedroom, probably preparing our breakfast. *"How I love him!"* I thought as I crept to the door and silently peeped out.

Kenneth was kneeling on the floor by a hard kitchen chair with his elbow resting on the seat. He covered his face with his hands in the endearing way he always had when he was embarrassed or emotional. I could hear his agonized confession and his prayer for forgiveness as he whispered them into his hands. I was peeking through the cracked door like some unwelcome intruder, again, gathering memories that weren't even meant for me. I knew now that he was truly committed, but not to me.

I silently closed the door and crawled back into bed. I pulled the covers over my head and wept bitter tears.

The dice were flung, they never reached the backboard, and they turned up … SNAKE EYES … I lose again … No more turns … move on, please!

"Are you awake, Faye?" Kenneth said softly from the bedroom door.

"Yes," I answered. "I am."

"I'm going out for a while. I'll bring our breakfast back with me," he said. "Do you have a preference?"

"No, I'll take potluck," I called back from under the covers, trying to sound normal.

"Yeah?" he asked.

"Yeah!" I answered.

When Kenneth was gone, I bathed and dressed and went to the kitchen to start a pot of coffee. I set out the milk and a few pieces of flatware. Then I waited with an uneasy feeling. *He has to come home sooner or later,* I thought, *he lives here.* A few minutes later I heard his key turn in the lock. "Did you wait long?"

"No, not really," I answered. "A little while, I guess."

"I'm sorry I took so long; I stopped at St. Anthony for a minute or two," he said as he kissed my head.

"No problem," I said, and I thought, *So you went "home" then?*

"Are you hungry?"

"Not too hungry, but I can eat something."

"Yeah?" he asked.

I ignored our familiar banter and tried to keep myself together. Last night we had been one flesh, and now we sat across the table with the Church between us. It was so painful I could barely swallow. *His scent is still in my nostrils,* I prayed silently. *God have mercy, let me have him!*

"What's bothering you, honey?" he asked, taking my hand. "Did I do something to upset you?"

"Kenneth, do you believe that I love you?" I asked.

"I know you do, and I love you. What's up?" he smiled.

"Kenneth, I want you to take more time to consider the priesthood. I'll wait for you, for as long as it takes. I don't want to marry you until you're really sure. I don't want the Church between us, Kenneth."

"Faye!" he cried, covering his face in his boyish way, "you heard me!"

I went to him and pulled him into my arms. "I love you," I said. "I'll always love you."

"I love you, too," he whispered. We had made a silent pact. We both knew at that moment that he was already committed to the priesthood, he would never be free, and that we would stay with each other until he had to leave. All through the summer and into fall we made love as though we were going to be together forever. Pretending! I was more sexual during this time than at any other time in my life, always feeling that I had to satiate my appetite for him before he was gone.

We talked into the night often about our love for each other and the prayers for happiness and fulfillment we had for each other. My love for him grew even stronger as our separation loomed, and I found myself clinging to the only part of him that was exclusively mine, our lovemaking. My body ached for him, and I took as much of him as I could before he left me. When I wasn't making love to him with my body, my mind was making love to him; *Come to me, Kenneth, and let me love you ... let me love you!* I prayed until my knees were calloused, worn out from praying, but the answer always came back to me the same: "Let him go!" In spite of that I continued to ask, *Why ... Why?*

Eventually Kenneth came to me and told me, with those soft lips that I loved so much, that he would have to go, and asked to be freed from his promise to me. I had to let him go because he was never really mine, but that didn't save my heart from breaking.

He went away to be ordained a priest and I ... I just stayed behind to twist in the wind. No Kenneth, no love, no hope! When we struck our bargain so many months before, I never imagined that I would have pain like this. It was breathtaking, it was so intense. I could find no refuge from it. I carried it with me wherever I went, night and day. I couldn't taste food, or enjoy humor, or hear music, and I couldn't sleep. My only sensation was one of loneliness and self-pity.

"Move on, you've had your turn ... Please, step away from the dice!"

How could my God do this to me? I didn't understand why he had to take this wonderful man from me. He had so many people, and I had but one. He knew I would never love again. He brought Kenneth to me, made me love him, and then snatched him away again. I accepted it because I had no choice, but I resented this cruel judgment, and I vowed I would resent it forever. I shall never forget the first morning I awoke to his absence.

The image of Kenneth haunted every inch of the office we once shared, and his absence was unbearable. Martin tried to cheer me up by accelerating our friendship with invitations to lunch and beer stops after work, but it didn't help. I think it made things worse.

One week after Kenneth left, I tendered my resignation and called Michael O'Leary.

I asked him if there was anything at all available so that I could get my foot in the door. "I'm not fussy, Michael," I said. "I will start wherever I have to, as long as it's in my field."

"Well, good!" he said. "I would like to get you on board here. I have to say, though, that I'm disappointed you didn't respond when we had an opening. I made every effort to have a dialogue with you then. I can't make any promises, but I'll see what I can dig up, Faye, and get back to you."

"I'll be honest with you, Michael," I said. "I've suffered a personal setback ... and then, as you probably know, Nick Beck is my biological father and with my face out there ... It hasn't been easy. So I've taken some time just to recover from the ordeal and get myself together. I can promise you, though—I'm fit and work ready now, if you'll have me," I lied.

Surprisingly, Michael called me the following week, and I started working for him. It was a good match. We worked well together. We were both good at our craft.

I threw myself into my work and stayed to myself. I had no interest in socializing with anyone, and it wasn't as if I was without human contacts; there were always people at my office, I reasoned, and there was always a glass or two of some adult beverage to take the edge off at night. Two or three was always better than one.

I avoided the Moon Café as I passed by it, turning my face away from the huge window in front, just in case someone would be standing there and look out at me. I wouldn't want him to see how pathetic I was.

When Kenneth and I parted, I kept his ring and wore it on a chain around my neck. It was the most valued possession I owned ... that and one of his shirts, permeated with his scent, that I had retrieved from the clothes hamper. I could press it to my face and inhale his fragrance clinging there. The eighteenth of June was our anniversary, the night he gave me his pledge. It was the loneliest night of the year for me.

That day, my phone rang. I answered it and no one spoke, so I asked, "Can you talk?"

There was a pause. "Yes, of course, do you want to talk?" the beautiful baritone voice on the other end said.

I answered, "I need to!"

There was another pause and then softly, "Yeah?"

"Yeah," I whispered.

It wasn't enough! It's never enough!

I was glad I had a two o'clock appointment with Amy Stein, my therapist, the day after that call, because I thought that I might be crashing emotionally. The call had opened old wounds. I had a few drinks before I went over to ease the emotional sting I was feeling.

I told her about the call I had from Kenneth and how I had wept for the love we still felt for each other and couldn't share. Instead of sympathizing with me, she unleashed a volley of accusations: "I would like to see you stop your damned drinking!" she admonished me. "And get it through your thick skull that you are not the only one who's ever been dumped!"

"Kenneth didn't dump me!" I said defensively.

"Faye, he dumped you, do you remember? Do you hear what I'm saying? You were dumped, probably because you were too needy. You probably smothered him into unconsciousness, and now he's gone. Move on! He won't be back! He's a priest!"

"Shut your fucking mouth, you quack!" My voice rose. "He loves me! You tried to keep us apart! I remember that!"

"Well, Faye, here are the facts. You can trivialize yourself with your petty self-pity, or you can have a life! It's your choice! You have a chance to live a full, courageous, self-fulfilled life, or you can sit and blubber over the past while life passes you by. Call it, Faye, call it! I can't get through to you, Faye. So far, you're a stinking disappointment, so get your sorry self out of my office, go home, and do your crying there!"

I sat for a moment, stunned, staring at her in disbelief. She stared back at me defiantly.

"You're the biggest bitch that ever lived, Amy! I'm through with you!" I said evenly, and I slammed the door behind me as I left.

"What're you looking at?" I snapped at the woman behind the desk. "Fuck you!"

I felt uncontrolled rage growing stronger by the minute. I can honestly say that I don't know how I got home. I can't remember a stoplight or a corner that I turned, but somehow I was putting my key into the lock, turning it, and entering my kitchen. I threw my keys on the table and poured a water glass full of Jack Daniels, put an ice cube in it, and added a squirt of Coke. I threw myself down in a big soft chair and drank it down. My mind was completely empty. I didn't want to know what she wanted me to hear.

I saw a brief that I was supposed to be working on at home lying on the table untouched, and I didn't give a shit if it ever got done. *To hell with everything,* I thought. I went into the kitchen and fixed myself another glass of the elixir.

"He didn't dump me, Goddamn it, it's not my fault!" I said aloud. "Fuck her!" I stormed and drank it down.

Morning found me in the same chair, rumpled and ill. "Stop your damned drinking," rang in my head, and I thought, *I have to stop drinking, that's for sure.*

Finally, with the help of my therapist, it was apparent even to me that I was indulging an obsession that was unhealthy and destructive, that the phone calls were wishful thinking and existed only in my imagination, a desperate release from an unbearable self-inflicted loneliness, not normal, separate, with differentness at my core. Indeed, it was not Kenneth who called me, with a tacit confession that he had made an error when he chose the priesthood, but I who had called him. It was he who had once loved me who tried to ease my pain by responding with loving concern and respect.

I had a hangover, and I was crashing emotionally. It seemed to me that life was not worth the humiliation one must endure to live it. There was no soft place to lie. The shame I felt was overwhelming, and my head was going to explode. So much for living a self-fulfilled life. I tried to find something that would settle my stomach and finally took a glass of milk. I finished it and picked up the phone.

"Hello, Amy, please don't hang up! I ... uh ... I may have been a little hasty yesterday. I would like to apologize for my inappropriate conduct. I ... uh ... want to see you, if I can ... if you're still available to me."

"Of course I am, Faye, let me see what times I have open for you."

Part Six

229

Chapter 32

The episode that I had suffered at Amy's hand seemed to be a turning point for me, tough as it was. Amy suggested that I make a few friends. "Go out and have some fun. You'll be surprised how interesting life can be if you actually live it. Get yourself something a little sexy to wear, you know, like a little black dress and shoes without laces!"

"I really think I dress quite appropriately," I countered.

"You dress well for work in a law office, but for an evening to remember you need something a little silky and slinky," she grinned. "Let yourself look a little vulnerable, live a little, but stay away from too many margaritas! And don't think you have to be in love, just have a little fun. Lighten up, and find some friends."

"I have no female friends other then you," I admitted. "You're my closest friend," I told her.

"Right," she said, drumming her pencil on the desk. "Wonderful! Okay, well, thank you, Faye ... anyway ... get some female friends, or go with male friends. Go to a show or something, for God's sake!"

"I hate to admit this, but I have no male friends either. The only friend I ever had ... you know ... I have no friends."

"I want you to set a goal for yourself to make a friend or two. That's your assignment." She smiled. "Faye, remember, you don't have to relive the past unless you want to. We talked about that ... remember?"

I left her office buoyed up, with the intention of having a new friend by the time I had my next appointment scheduled—and I did try to find someone who I could approach with an invitation to do some recreational activity of some kind. It made me feel like a stalker, always waiting and watching.

This was definitely not my strength, trying to scare up meaningless conversation with someone who probably couldn't give a shit about anything I had to say anyway.

I told Amy at my next session with her that I hadn't been able to make a connection with anyone. "I wish I knew how to make friends, but I have a problem with that."

"Be open to it and available, that's all. It won't be a problem for you. I want you to work on this, Faye."

As time passed, I relaxed my search for friends and went back to my old routine. I was finding it harder and harder to resist my urge to bring Kenneth's shirt to my face. I fought the voice inside me that repeated *Kenneth ... Kenneth!* I re-dedicated myself daily to the quest for a "full, courageous, self-fulfilled life." Give me a break Amy!

The possibilities of having a friend and not knowing it are slim to none, especially when you're hell-bent on finding one, but it turned out that I already had a friend in Michael O'Leary. I didn't think of him as a friend at all; I thought of him as my boss. I didn't count the times that Michael and I had stopped for coffee on the way to a deposition, or tried a new café for lunch, or walked together discussing the pros and cons of a case.

I didn't count it as a friendship because I never imagined that he thought of me as a friend. I thought he did things with me because it was an office duty. After all, I knew that as county prosecutor, he met with and lunched with many people, male and female.

To me it was all part of the job. I certainly would not have had the audacity to ask him to befriend me in some social or recreational capacity. I never really counted Michael as a possibility in my quest for companionship. He never showed even the slightest interest in socializing with me. He was just there doing his job and caring for his two little girls since the death of his wife four years earlier. He spent his evenings at home with his girls and took his work home with him. That was his life.

Hanna was his oldest daughter and resembled her father with her brown hair and huge, crazy green eyes. She was eight years old, just going into the gawky stage. The other girl was six-year-old Krista. She had dark hair that curled around her chubby cupid's face. Her eyes were a dark brown to match her dark hair. She must have looked like her mother. Michael called both girls by the same name: "Sweetie."

Sometimes he complained that his two dogs were driving him crazy. A huge golden lab called Sandy and a sad-eyed beagle named Woofs that his girls invited up on the furniture when he wasn't watching. He often had to ask me to brush hair from his back before a court appearance or some other function where dog hair was not acceptable.

"Could you check my back for dog hair, Faye? My Sweeties like to have Sandy and Woofs on the furniture when I'm not watching. Sometimes I forget to remain standing until I leave the house," he laughed.

Then it just happened: after one of our cases where the verdict could have gone either way but came down in our favor, Michael grabbed me and danced me around the office with the staff applauding us, some of them joining us.

"I can't dance," I objected.

"C'mon," he laughed, "I'll teach you."

That's when I decided to seize the moment. "That sounds like fun," I said. "Call me anytime."

I heard the dice clatter away, heard them slam into the backboard and turn … I held my breath.

"You mean it?" he asked.

"What do you think?" I smiled.

He nodded his head. "Okay, I'll do that! I'll call you."

SEVENS! … I win!

I couldn't wait to tell Amy that I had completed my assignment. I was proud that I put myself out there, a courageous effort to find a friend. Even if it never pans out, and we never go dancing, I thought I'd made a good-faith attempt to live a self-fulfilled life. I was elated … and shocked the following Wednesday when Michael actually called. "I have a sitter for Saturday, Faye. How's about we go dancing?"

"It sounds great," I said and asked, "Doesn't it concern you in the least that I don't know how to dance?"

"I'm going to give you a lesson," he laughed. After exchanging a few work-related thoughts, Michael told me that he would make reservations at the Rose Room for dinner at seven and pick me up at six-thirty or slightly before. I told him that would be great, and we rang off.

I dialed Amy and asked her if she thought it would be appropriate for me to wear the black dress I had purchased when she first gave me the assignment to get some eveningwear and find some friends. I couldn't wait until our next appointment; I wanted her to know immediately that I was successful!

"Of course, it would be exactly right. You're going for dinner and dancing, you need the slinky stuff," Amy said.

"You do know this guy is my boss?" I quizzed.

Amy came back, "He is a man, isn't he?"

"Oh yeah, definitely," I affirmed.

"Then put your make-up on, wear your slinky stuff, be a lady, and limit yourself to two drinks, plus one glass of wine with dinner. Got it?" she asked. "Faye, don't fall in love, take your time."

"I have it!" I told her and rang off. I dialed my beautician and made an appointment for my hair and make-up at four. That would give me time to get dressed and be ready to go at six. Amy was right, living life could be fun!

At six o'clock, Michael tapped lightly on my door, barely audible. When I answered the door, I was pleasantly surprised. He was dressed for a special occasion, fit to kill, and he looked so fine! I felt my antenna go up a bit. I could tell that this wasn't a throwaway date. It was special. It was a Michael I hadn't seen before. He definitely looked interested now. I loved it when he looked at me. "Whoa!" he said, "Hello, beautiful! Do you know if Faye Lawrence lives around here?"

"Get out, Michael!" I giggled, feeling a little foolish for my reaction. The dance lesson was more than I had imagined it could be. We danced close and slow in the dimly lit club. The evening was joyous, and conversation was easy. He kissed me goodnight at my door. It took my breath away, and I felt guilty later because I wanted him more than I should have. The thrill was definitely there, even though I tried to deny it. I thought it wasn't fair to Kenneth to desire someone else like that, but somehow I didn't care that much anymore. It had been a long time. I liked the feeling. Why resist?

Michael leaned against the door sill, his legs crossed and his elbow on the sill, his handsome face resting against his fist. "May I come in for a while?" he asked.

"Maybe next time," I answered.

I heard the dice clattering away again, bam! Into the backboard ... I held my breath!

"Can we plan something for next weekend, Faye?"

ELEVEN! ... I win again!

"Maybe we could have dinner and see a flick, or ... dance, or something?" he asked.

"Sure, that sounds like fun, and I think I'm free next Saturday. I'll let you know," I told him, as if I needed a calendar for my social life. What a joke!

"Goodnight, dancer," he said. I watched him soft-shoe his way down the hall.

"'Night," I called after him. It was a night to remember. I was taking charge of my destiny, just like that. I was living a self-fulfilling life with courage. It was good to have a friend, a special friend, and it was just the beginning of something more beautiful than I could ever have imagined. He was a perfect fit for me!

When we realized that we were in love, we began spending much of our time with his children. We would grill our dinner outdoors sometimes, and at other times I would attempt to cook something, usually with catastrophic results, or we would order takeout and sit around the table in the formal dining room, since the table in the kitchen was usually filled with papers and briefs that Michael was working on.

One evening, after we had finished eating outdoors, Michael ran into the kitchen to get some ice cream for us. Krista took the opportunity to let me know that she didn't like me anymore.

I was surprised to hear that, because of the two girls I had always thought she was the most receptive to me.

"Why don't you like me anymore?" I asked her.

"Because you made Dad take my mom's picher down when you came here," she frowned. "I want to look at my mom's picher."

"I don't think I asked him to take it down, Krista. Maybe he took it down to have it cleaned," I told her.

"Dad told me that Mom's picher made you uncomferble. He packed it away," she charged.

"Well, I'll tell your dad that I'm not uncomfortable, and maybe he will put it back. Could we be friends again then, Krista?"

"You better!" she frowned.

Mom's picture was restored to its original place, never to be moved again, and I regained a lifelong friend in my Krista. She was a loving little girl, and very easy to love.

Michael's first wife's name was Hillary. She was beautiful with dark features like those of Krista. I often stood before her and silently thanked her for this wonderful family that she had left for me. I prayed for her eternal happiness every night.

Michael took me dancing regularly. We would dress to the hilt and dance the night away. Michael loved to dance, and I soon loved it as well.

Michael and I played squash a couple of times a week. A game like tennis but on a smaller scale, where you slam the ball into the wall with your racket and your partner has to do the same on the rebound until one of you can't return it. We had fierce matches that left us both exhausted and sweaty. We loved these wild games because we were both fiercely competitive.

We stopped regularly after work to visit my apartment, making love together to the throaty strains of a saxophone blowing some jazz music that Michael had brought over. He was a perfect friend and a breathtaking lover.

When he brought me home after dancing, he would always kiss me goodnight at the door then he would ask, "May I come in for a while?" I always permitted him to enter because I wanted … needed … his lovemaking and the sound of that wailing sax. *Blow it baby … make it cry!*

Our lives were full and happy. My family loved Michael. He and Uncle Paul talked for hours and took long walks in the woods while I spent time with my mother and Patty catching up on family news.

They always had news about Sharon, now in the seventh grade in school and of Charl, who lived and worked in New York. He remained a bachelor, his handsome face appearing on the evening news as an anchor.

Hanna and Krista loved visiting the country. They would poke around happily discovering the wonders of nature, or they would follow Michael and Paul as they walked slowly along talking.

Chapter 33

Willie didn't return to his family but chose to wander the world as a Marine. He called my mother once in a great while to tell her that she shouldn't worry about him and to ask if Uncle Paul still knew where his fingertip was buried. He had no idea how much pain he had caused his family and probably didn't worry about it too much if he did.

Willie surprised everybody when he and his friend Matt visited the family ranch unannounced. My mother called me with her voice out of control. "You better get out here," she said. "Your brother's here. He's come home!"

"Which brother is home, Mom?" I quizzed.

"Your brother Willie, that's who! He's here right now!" she said, excitement building in her voice.

"May I talk to him, Mom?" I asked.

"He's right here, so you can talk away," she chirped.

"Hello?" a man's voice said.

"Willie?" I asked.

"How in hell are you, babe?" he asked. "Jesus! It's good to hear your voice."

"Willie," I sniveled. "Willie, you're really home?"

"Yeah, I ... I guess so ... for a while anyway," he choked but quickly recovered his swagger. "Why don't you drive yourself out here to see me?"

"I will, Willie. I'll arrange it for tonight if I can, which is doubtful. If not, I'll see you tomorrow early."

"Okay, sis, late tonight doubtful or tomorrow for sure then ... okay?"

"I love you, Willie," I told him.

"Shut your face now, babe, before you get me started," he chuckled. "I'll see you tomorrow or late tonight then?"

"I'll be there, Willie."

"Oh my God! I'll be waiting."

I called Michael and told him the good news that Willie was home for a visit. I told him that I would like him and the girls to come with me to visit Willie. "I want you to meet him, Michael," I said.

"I wouldn't have it any other way, sweetie. You make the arrangements. We can take the girls out of school for a couple days, and we'll all go up. I miss Uncle Paul and your mom anyway."

"Michael, I'm going to book accommodations in Fenwick, because Willie brought a friend with him so I'm sure the house will be full, especially if Charl comes home to see Willie. Charl probably wouldn't stay at the ranch if he brings a friend, but just in case."

"You take care of it, sweetie; I'll go wherever you lead me. I have a few things to clean up here. Can we go in the morning?"

"It sounds good; I'll get on it."

"Yeah, baby! That's an affirmative," he laughed.

I made reservations for us to stay in a motel in Fenwick for two days and arrangements with the school for the girls to take a few days off. The school refused my request pending a call from Michael to confirm taking them out of school. I assured them that he would call. I called Michael back and told him that he would have to call the school. "I'm just going to have to marry you so you can take care of this stuff," he laughed.

"It sounds good to me," I said.

The girls were elated when they found that they were taking time away from their lessons to visit the ranch. We packed our things that evening so that we could be ready to leave early in the morning, and we drove into the morning sun with our shades on and the visor pulled down.

We arrived in Fenwick, checked into our motel, and unloaded our bags. We stopped at the truck stop for breakfast but didn't linger over our coffee, pushing on quickly, anxious to reach the ranch. Finally we were gliding along between the two white board fences that lined the driveway to my beloved adopted home and the dear ones who waited there. Michael pulled the car up to the front door and stopped. The first person to appear in the doorway was my Willie. He held his huge arms open, and I flung the car door open and ran into them.

We stood like that embracing one another and crying tears of joy. "Oh, Willie, I love you … I love you," I told him.

"Shhhh, babe, I know," he whispered. "I love you too … so now you made me bawl again … men don't bawl," he laughed, pawing at his eyes with the back of his hand.

Michael and the girls stood by waiting for Willie and me to unlock our arms, and when we finally did Michael stepped forward, extending his hand. I introduced Michael and the girls to Willie. He told them that he preferred Will to Willie. "Willie was fine when I was a little boy," he said. The three of us talked for a bit, but before we knew it, the rest of the family pressed in around us in a din of voices and laughter.

When Will had gone to join the Marines, he had been a big chubby kid, but he returned a confident Marine. He had obviously worked for his excellent physique. His auburn hair was clipped close to his head, and his face looked freshly scrubbed. He could have been a commercial to recruit Marines. He introduced his friend Matthew Forbes. He had the same clean and tidy look. He too was trim and muscular. "This is my buddy, Matt," Will said.

Uncle Paul was beside himself; he couldn't take himself away from Willie. He delighted in the hubbub of family. He was an attentive host, always trying to bring things or pull up chairs for everyone.

The first day we were there, Uncle Paul, Willie and I drove to the Gethsemane Cemetery and Paul pointed out the family plot and the stone with Will's name on it. The date was missing, to be filled in later.

WILLARD JAMES LAWRENCE
"Beloved Son and Friend"

"It's in there, son, no worries. I had them put it in deep enough so that when the time comes to open the grave, it won't be disturbed," he said, his eyes welling up. Willie took Uncle Paul in his arms, and they cried together to heal the years of separation.

"You called me son, Uncle Paul," Will said.

"Yes, if you permit me that, I've loved you like a son, Will."

"Thank you, I'll always remember you as my dad... I love you too."

On the last day of our visit, Willie came to me and asked if the two of us could slip away and take a walk or something. "God only knows when I'll get home again. I just want to talk; I want to know what's been going on with you," he said.

I was anxious to know about his life, too. "Let's just walk to the creek; that would be a nice walk. Let's go right now. That way we can be back in time for dinner," I suggested.

"Sounds good," he said.

Uncle Paul and Michael had gone for a walk earlier, and the girls were with them, so it was a good time for Will and me to steal away together. Will asked Matt if he would mind staying alone while he took a walk with his sister, and Matt agreed to stay back with Patty and Mom.

We talked about Pops being captured at the ranch. Even though Will had already been filled in by the rest of the family, I thought for some reason he should hear my version. I told him how I had loved and lost and then miraculously found my true love in Michael. How we lived a life filled with joy. How perfect we were for each other and that I thought we might be married someday.

He told me about the places he had traveled, the adventures he had while he was gone, and the friends he had made in the military. "We're career Marines," he said. "It's a brotherhood of misfits, like me."

"Are you happy, Willie … Will?" I asked.

"All things considered … sometimes, you know, I am … right now I am," he beamed.

"All things considered?" I quizzed.

"Yeah, well, you know, sometimes things catch up with me a little … I guess. I wasn't raised in a monastery, you know?"

"I've been seeing a shrink for a long time now," I confided. "It really has helped me sort through some anger problems and other problems I was having. I had everything … anger, booze, and a sexual obsession for a while. Have you ever considered going that route, Will?"

"You mean the sexual obsession route?" he laughed.

"You know what I mean … the shrink route."

"I don't think so. I can't believe it would help with my problems, Faye. I'll have mine until they throw dirt in my face," he said.

"I'm sorry, Will. I wish you would try it. I didn't think it would help me either, but believe me, it did."

"I don't know, Faye, I'll think about it," Will shrugged.

"It breaks my heart when I think of everything. Why did Pops want to kill you that night, Will?" I asked him.

"You don't want to know, Faye, let it go," he said.

"I don't want to let it go, I want to know! It's important for me to understand why. It has always been a secret, and I need to know why," I said. "I've always felt responsible for some reason, Will."

"Okay, do you remember the Christmas that you got the shit beat out of you for trying to resist him? Well, he was jealous of me because of you, he thought we were lovers," he confided.

We had been holding hands, sitting in the grass overlooking a beautiful little valley that fell down to the creek below. When he told me why the assault happened, I jerked my hand away and jumped to my feet. "My God, Willie," I said, "don't say that! Lovers! Why Will? Why did he think we were lovers?"

"Because I had made a gift for you, and he found it.

"A gift, what was it?" I asked.

"It was a little heart I carved out of wood and a few pieces of candy I saved from the Christmas party."

"Oh Willie, thank you! I would have loved my gift, and I'm sorry that you got in trouble because of it!"

"I had written 'Willie and Franny' on the back of the heart. That's all it took! I didn't mean anything by it. I just wanted you to know I loved you," he said, but when he looked at me, the admission of guilt was on his face. "Faye, I guess I've always loved you ... maybe the wrong way when I was a kid ... I don't know. I was a young boy in the throes of puberty, and I was fucked up by everything. I knew the old man was doing ... things to you. I couldn't stand it. I hated that old bastard and loved him at the same time."

"Willie, I think what you felt was a natural reaction to all the craziness around you when you were a boy; you were trying to find something comforting in life. We were never taught about boundaries, and I did cling to you, you were all I had," I told him.

"There were never any boundaries!" Will said. "I'm sorry, but that's why he did it. He found the gift." Will had remained seated and looked up at me; his eyes were filled with that profound sadness I'd seen so often. Shrugging his shoulders, he said simply, "You asked, babe."

"Will," I said, "please don't tell me that I caused you to have an unhappy life! I never wanted to … I never meant to at all!"

"You didn't cause anything. We had a tough go of it, both of us did, but I'm still messed up, Faye. I have a lot of problems; loving you is not one of them. A lot of it's my fault … I don't trust anybody. You have to know I'm not like the old man, but I still have my moments." Will rose and stood over me. "C'mon let's go back," he said, "none of this is helpful, it's bad stuff!"

"Don't go, please," I begged. "I'm afraid we won't be the same after this."

"Nothing has changed, Faye, we're always going to be the same. I love you, you're my sister."

When we got back, I put my arms around Willie, before we joined the others, and kissed him. "Hold me, Willie, I miss that! Write to me, too," I whispered, "and I'll write to you. I love you, my sweet brother, I always will."

"I'll hold you in my dreams, babe, Semper Fi," he whispered, holding me and rocking from side to side. "Go on now and have a life!" He turned his back to me. "Give me a minute or two alone, I gotta let go!" he said. I went inside and cried a little in the bathroom. Matt asked me where Will was when I came out, and when I told him, he went to Will. I joined Michael and the others, but Will and Matt stayed back with their thoughts.

That was the last time I saw Will. He wrote me a few times, and then the letters stopped, and he dropped away from all family connections. I continued writing him, but my letters were returned, "Addressee Unknown."

I tried to locate him, but I found that he hadn't re-enlisted in the Marines when his hitch was up for some mysterious reason. I continued to look for him and discovered he had been incarcerated for assault. He refused my calls and went underground. He was in and out of jail from time to time. I tried to track him from jail to jail, but I lost him and finally had to let him go.

His soul had been injured when he was a child, and he had fallen under the hand of evil that was forced on him. There was nothing I could do to save him. I struggled to overcome the old anger and hatred that fought to take my heart back. Prayer was my only defense.

Somewhere in North Dakota, there's a gravestone engraved:

WILLARD JAMES LAWRENCE
"Beloved Son and Friend"

Buried deep beneath it, the tip of my sweet Willie's finger rests. It waits for an unknown date in the future when it will be united with its bruised and battered host ... if he finds his way home again.

Chapter 34

Michael and I were married in a private ceremony held in the backyard at Michael's house. My mother, Sharon, Uncle Paul, Patty, and their children were in attendance. Charl was there with his handsome face and a beautiful woman named Macy on his arm. His breath smelled of booze. He hadn't escaped unscathed either ... *hang on, Charl, get help and fight it!* I thought. Michael's father, Benjamin, flew in from Florida. That was the first time I met him. He had lost his wife, Michael's mother, to cancer eight years earlier. His hair was white, and his shoulders were stooped with arthritis. When he embraced Michael, his eyes welled up with emotion.

Hanna and Krista stood with us as we took our vows. Each one had written a statement to read for the ceremony, fidgeting and stammering as they delivered them in their nice dresses, holding bouquets.

Krista's message was short:

Dad said to welcome you, Faye.
You can come and live with us.
You can come in my room sometimes.
Happy Wedding, Dad and Faye.

Next Hanna recited her poem:

> *Your wedding day is today,*
> *I'm glad for Dad and Faye*
> *I hope that God will bless today.*
> *And everything will be okay.*
> *Happy Wedding, Dad and Faye.*

Our eyes were damp when they read these lines. Michael had done a wonderful job raising both of his children to be loving and honest. I loved them; we both loved them.

Michael offered to move to a new home for us, one that would be ours alone, but I wasn't in favor of that. I loved his place, and I didn't want to disrupt the girls' lives. I didn't want to take Hillary's picture down. We liked to look at Mom's picture.

I moved my things into Michael's home in the days preceding our wedding, but I stayed at my apartment until our wedding vows were taken. Michael thought that would be best for the girls, and I agreed.

We kept my apartment open after we were married, just for the two of us. We'd steal away often to take an afternoon together listening to Michael's jazz music and making love, as lovers do, without consideration for anyone but ourselves.

We celebrated our wedding reception at the Rose Room restaurant where we had our first date. We invited our families, of course, and people from our office, Dr. Amy Stein and her husband, Mr. and Mrs. Martin Jacobson, and Ernie Cranston. It was a beautiful candlelit affair with clinking glasses raised in toasts, dancing, and good will all around.

Ernie and my mother spent the evening huddled together, talking and laughing. It made my heart warm to see them enjoying each other and celebrating together. I entertained the idea that they could have filled two lonely lives with joy if only … If only it could have been … Oh well.

I was particularly glad to see Amy there. She told me that she was proud of me and that she would like to meet for lunch sometime soon. I accepted her invitation and told her I would call her when we were back from our honeymoon. "Promise now, and don't forget," she said.

"I definitely will call you, Amy," I promised. "We both know you are my closest female friend, right?"

"The more things change, the more they stay the same, Faye," she answered. "Make sure you call me when you get home. I want to meet you socially for a change."

We arranged for members of our family to care for our children while we were away, and we stayed the first night of our married life at our apartment. Dancing together in our open robes, swaying to the heady jazz music Michael had brought over, feeling our oneness and moving together, ever closer to a mutual submission to our growing libidos and the plaintive strains of that throaty saxophone.

We made tender love to one another on our wedding night, our night, and added our own promises to those we had given before the priest. "Bone of my bone and flesh of my flesh, Faye," Michael whispered.

"Bone of your bone and flesh of your flesh," I pledged. My heart was so full of love for him ... *Michael, Michael, my true love, my sweet husband!*

Michael asked me later if I could consider calling him some endearing name, like dear, or honey, or sweetheart now and then. "You're so formal with me," he complained. "You do know I'm your husband now, don't you?" he said, looking at me quizzically with his insanely beautiful hazel-green eyes.

"It's difficult for me to do, because there was never much of that as I was growing up, unless I was going to be the victim of a sexual assault or something," I laughed.

He grabbed me in a rough hug and slammed my body to his. "I'm sorry, sweetie, I didn't think! You can call me 'hey you'! That's okay."

"There is no sound sweeter than your precious name, Michael," I confessed. "But I do have one special name I would like to call you on occasion. How does 'doofus' strike you?" I teased.

"Michael will do," he laughed. "Now that you've explained it that way, Michael sounds okay!"

We took only one glorious week to celebrate our honeymoon, partially because of a pressing case he was prosecuting and partially because of the siren call of family life. One day at lunch, we talked and decided that the girls should help us celebrate, so we packed up and surprised them by coming home early. They were elated, and so were we. We took a five-day trip up along the north shore by Duluth, Minnesota. It was glorious! That was the first time Krista ever came to me, hugging me around my hips and turning her face up to me. She was beginning to trust me, and I loved both of the girls.

When we were at home, we always thought of getting away from the chaos, but when we were away, we craved the warmth of family. A joyous mixture of voices, footsteps, and wagging tails, finding socks, and cooking pancakes with bacon, of catching school pageants and recitals, of barking dogs … and of prenatal care appointments. We savored all of the things that make up the richness of family life.

Our son, Paul Benjamin O'Leary, was welcomed into our family with unbridled joy. He was a beautiful, happy child who stole the hearts of our girls and completed Michael and me. My Uncle Paul was delighted that he had been honored with a namesake. "This is a tremendous honor you've bequeathed me," he said with his eyes welling up at the christening. "I have been blessed!" he said, holding his hat behind his back, his chin quivering.

Michael added me to his list of "sweeties" so that when he calls for Sweetie, sometimes we all answer—but he calls his boy Buddy. "We men must stick together, right, Buddy? Atta boy! You're the man, Buddy," he would tell him, and Paul would turn his face up to him mesmerized.

Michael would sit at the kitchen table so that he could be in the midst of the hubbub, with his papers and briefs strewn before him, his glasses worn below his eyes and his coffee always within arm's length. How I loved him!

His children were always around him. They came to him and leaned on his shoulder or teased him when he was busy or told him to look at something they were doing. "Look, Dad, look at me. Look! Dad, did you see me?"

Hanna and Krista attend parochial school at our church, so when Father Murphy was transferred to our parish, even though I was extremely uncomfortable with it, I couldn't ask Michael to change parishes and uproot the girls, so I said nothing.

I didn't welcome watching Father Murphy's homilies, for obvious reasons. I was afraid that I would entertain memories that would infringe somehow on the beautiful love that Michael and I shared. I wished that I had told Michael about Kenneth, especially about the call I had received from him after Michael and I had fallen in love, but I hadn't. Another reason was that when I first dated Michael, I had thought that the only problem with him was that he wasn't Kenneth! When Michael and I first became involved, I used to ask myself, "If Kenneth were to leave the priesthood and ask me to come back to him, would I run back?"

I had gotten the definitive answer to this question a few months before Michael and I were married, when Kenneth called me suffering a crisis in his commitment to the priesthood. My heart stopped at the sound of his voice.

"Faye, it's me," he said. "Martin tells me you're going to marry Michael O'Leary?"

"I am, Kenneth," I told him.

"I called to wish you the best. I'm happy for you," he said.

"I'm very happy. Thank you," I said.

"It hasn't been that long, Faye. I mean … since we called it quits. I know it's crazy but I thought you would always be there."

"Kenneth, it's been over three years,"

"It's just that you promised to wait, does he love you, I mean ... more than I do... did?" He asked.

"Yes, and even if he didn't and I were still available, you would never be. You know that, you were already taken ... before I met you."

"I thought I could make an impact as a priest but it's ... it's soul-crushing right now for me, Faye."

"I'm sorry, Kenneth," I told him, "try to be patient, you're doing what you were born to do; it's your destiny, you know that! You were chosen for this life and you said yourself that it wouldn't be easy, you knew that going in. It wasn't easy for me either. It'll get better, I just know it will, and you know it too, don't you?"

"I know my last chance with you has passed me now, honey, and I need to know if he loves you as much as I loved you."

"Kenneth, don't do this!"

"Does he love you as much?" he asked, does he think about you day and night?"

"I'm sorry, Kenneth."

"Does he treat you better?" he asked, "I hope he's good to you, I hope he treats you right!"

"Please don't do this Kenneth," I said, "I'm sorry, I won't lie to you ... he gave himself to me completely ... I can't do this, Kenneth, I belong to Michael, this is wrong!"

After a long silence, he said, "Maybe I can close the book on this part of my life then. God bless you both and your marriage, Faye, I mean that with all my heart."

"Thank you, Kenneth," I said. "I pray that God will bless you and give you the strength to carry on and peace. I'll always hold you in my prayers ... always! I do love you still."

"And I you, honey, more than you'll ever know!" he said. "Say goodbye, love."

"Goodbye, love," I answered. It was heartbreaking to hear him like this, because I loved him so much, and I felt almost selfish to have found my perfect completion in Michael, while Kenneth still struggled to fulfill his destiny. It had been a long, hard-fought battle. At one time I didn't think I could live without him, didn't think I would ever love anyone but Kenneth, then Michael came along and the love I held for Kenneth was eclipsed. I don't know why, but that was heartbreaking to me, it was as though it demeaned Kenneth in some way, especially when I heard his voice break. I had experienced how much it hurts to loose in love. The memory of that emotion was still vivid. I remembered ... "us" ... all of it, the bitter ... and the sweet!

I still wished someone else would say the Mass every Sunday. I was afraid that somehow an obstacle would be placed between Michael and me from seeing him so much, maybe his scent or his voice. I loved and wanted Michael alone, but I harbored a guilty conscience because I hadn't told Michael about Kenneth, and I held a curiosity about what life would have been like with Kenneth. Unthinkable traitorous thoughts ... again!

Self-loathing began to fester in my mind, and I started to avert my eyes when Michael looked at me. All too soon, the first Sunday that Father Murphy would say the Mass was upon us. The girls were dressed, Michael was ready to go, and I couldn't avoid it any longer—so I took Paul in my arms, gave my bag to Hanna to hold for me, and we left the house.

When we arrived at the church, Michael herded us into a pew in the middle of the church on the aisle. The music swelled, and the altar servers led the precession in.

Father Murphy swept in behind them in his opulent vestments of royal green brocade, heavily embroidered with rich gold, a satin scarf and white under-frock. He was an impressive figure sweeping along the aisle.

He mounted the altar, turning to look back at his flock; he made the sign of the cross with his arm. "In the name of the Father and the Son and the Holy Spirit," he said. His voice like satin, pure, baritone, and huge, filled the church. I felt a distinct pain in my heart at hearing his voice for the first time in this setting. There had been sacrifices made for this moment, huge sacrifices, and not by him alone. There was also pride in having contributed my share to the sacrifice. It was unwelcome but undeniable. I loved him still; it would never change.

When it was time for his homily, he stepped down from the altar and strode among the parishioners.

"I am going to ask you a question," he began, "and I want you to give this question a lot of thought before you answer it." He paused. "I don't want you to give me the answer … I want you to answer it for yourself."

"Here's the question," he said. "If it was against the law to have faith in Jesus Christ, and you were arrested for believing, would you be convicted … or would the charges be dropped because of reasonable doubt? Think about that!" He asked again, "Would you get off because of reasonable doubt … or would you be found guilty as charged?" He paused, looking back at the congregation.

"You need to be found guilty!" His voice rose. "Reject reasonable doubt!" he said. "You either believe ... or you don't believe! No middle ground! Think about it! You can't have it both ways.

"I'll ask you another question: Are you guilty of being a Catholic ... or do you simply attend Mass at the Catholic Church? Do you believe all the tenets the Catholic Church teaches, or do you choose the things that are convenient to believe in?

"Look in the back of the pew in front of you and find the menu the Church has provided for you there ... you can't find it? Then I have to confess that the Church doesn't offer you a menu to choose from. Instead, the Church offers you an opportunity to embrace her and all she stands for, all of her traditions, her doctrines ... without reservation! You have no standing to say 'I want this. I reject that!' The sacred doctrines of the Church are tested by time ... not worn out ... not negotiable!" he declared. "Drink the full cup or drink none of it! These tenets are provided to guide the faithful to the gates of heaven! Confused? That's all right, you're here to learn, and the Church is here to teach.

"Indulge me, I have yet another question: Does your neighbor know you are a committed Catholic? Your co-worker ... does he, or she know?" he asked, barely audible, "or are you afraid they will disapprove? Are you afraid to be seen with your Savior? Do you say, 'Yes, I am a Christian,' or do you give your approval to secularism by your silence? Be careful," he warned, shaking his head slowly, "make sure you kneel to worship the right God ... The only true God, the God of our fathers ... lest he say in the last hour ... 'I know you not!'" He paused for several moments and then continued quietly, "You either have faith or you do not. You are either a Catholic or you are not. Christ disdains a tepid soul. Choose a side!"

He turned and ascended the altar. The congregation was silent as he walked to the podium. "There's good news for all of us sinners," he said, turning to the crucifix and raising both arms to the crucified Christ. "The word made flesh!" he announced. "That's the good news! He will shelter you in his wounds ... He will hear you on the day that you call him!"

He crossed the altar to the ornate throne reserved for priests alone and sat down.

I understood that Kenneth could never have resisted his calling to the priesthood. He had been given these words, and he had to speak them. The message was for him as well as the parishioners. "Choose a side," he said, "drink the full cup or drink nothing!" Being ordained a priest hadn't made him immune to weakness or temptation. He had chosen a difficult, almost impossible, way of life! Three years after his ordination, he had reached a point of crises in his obligation. I can attest to that, because he came to me, the one who loved him, in desperation. I gave him comfort and encouragement as he had me when I was desperate.

I don't have to understand your methods, Lord, I thought, but you were right in the end. We are all where we should be, Kenneth at your altar and me with Michael and my family. I once wondered why you sent Kenneth to me only to snatch him away, but now I know I would never have sought help for my problems without him as the prize for doing it. I would not have had my dear ones, my family, my sweet Michael. You answered my prayers in your own way … I know that's the best way.

Father Murphy stood, led the congregation in prayer, and prepared the Eucharist. The music swelled. People filled the aisles, surging forward to receive communion from him, our new fire-and-brimstone priest. Michael with Paul in his arms, Hanna, Krista, and I stood in line waiting for our turn. When it was my turn, I stepped before Father Murphy. He raised the Eucharistic wafer. Our eyes met and exchanged our secret. "The body of Christ!" he told me. I bowed. "Amen," I agreed. He brought the wafer down, resting his little finger on my chin and carefully placing the treasure on my tongue.

I took one step to my left ready to make the sign of the cross and looked up at the soaring crucifix with a life-sized Jesus hanging there. I knelt as the warmth of Christ's love tumbled down on me. His spirit surrounded me. I was overwhelmed by the immensity of his love.

My father, as he had been when I last saw him, appeared to me, broken and bleeding. I had already forgiven him. I was finally free of him! I felt Michael touch my arm, and I rose and turned to let him lead me back to our family.

Later in the car, Michael asked, "Eat out or go home?"

"Home," I said. "Is that all right girls?"

"All right, Faye," they answered. "Home."

Michael rested his arm on the back of the seat massaging my neck with his fingers as we drove along. "Faye, I know about him and everything. I need to know if everything's good now, sweetie … I mean, are you all right?" he asked.

"Michael," I said, "it's all good. He didn't have a choice … he didn't choose, he was chosen. We're all where we should be … and anyway, I thank God he dumped me; if he hadn't, I would never have had you to love, and the kids. What could be better than that?"

"Nothing, sweetie, that's for sure!" he smiled and pulled me to himself. "It was a rotten deal, that's all I have to say."

"How did you know?" I asked.

"Marty Jacobson called me on your behalf and told me all about it before I ever hired you; as a matter of fact, that's one of the reasons I decided to give you another chance—well, that, and I sort of liked you a lot. I figured you already had enough heartache for this lifetime. Marty was mad as hell at Murphy for the lousy deal he gave you, sweetie. No matter how you slice it, it stinks."

"Daaad, you said H E double toothpicks, and that's not nice!" Krista admonished.

Michael made a face, "I'm sorry, sweetie. Tell Jesus, will you?" he said and then whispered, "Turn the radio up, Faye."

"Don't do it any more, Dad!" Krista threatened, "or I'll tell him you did it again!"

"I won't, sweetie," Michael promised, tapping me on the shoulder. "It's still a lousy deal," he insisted quietly. "Why do you defend him? I still think it stinks and he's a louse! Don't forget, I was the one who watched your heart breaking a little more every day."

"I didn't think you ever noticed me then, but I know you were the one that was there for me, and I know you were the one that really saved me Michael … I know that," I said. "We need to clear this up; I don't want secrets between us. Maybe we could have an apartment date after breakfast. I want to explain something I kept from you, and especially why I kept my relationship with him a secret when I knew very well that he was being transferred to our parish."

"That would be good ... maybe we can talk it out then," he said in a half whisper. "I would never have pushed it had he not been assigned to our parish, but I couldn't even take Communion. I had to step out of line because I was so full of anger, it was an awful feeling; I wanted to punch him in the face when he gave you Communion. Maybe I am a little ... I just don't understand why you defend him! That's what gets me more than anything ... you defend him! Why? Damn it anyway," he said, "and it still ... stinks!"

"I don't smell anything, Dad," Hanna said.

"I thought I smelled something, maybe not. I can't smell it anymore. Can you, sweetie?" Michael asked.

"I don't smell it anymore either," I said.

Hanna said, "I never smelled it at all."

"I hope you never do, sweetie, because it really smells to high heaven," he said, giving me a meaningful look to drive his point across.

When we got home, Hanna and I changed into our casual clothes and started breakfast. I mixed up some pancakes, and Hanna broke eggs into a bowl for scrambles while Michael entertained Paul and Krista. The dogs whined in wild anticipation, banging their tails on things.

All my loved ones watched me; their faces were turned toward me, all eyes were on my face. The stack of pancakes and the pan of bacon were almost ready. When I brought them, they'd dig in like hungry little wolves. I wondered what their futures held. What kind of young women would our girls be, and what would Paul choose in adulthood? Would he be an attorney like his father, a rancher like his namesake, or a priest …? *Please, God, let him be an attorney or a rancher, life is difficult enough.*

"Hanna, could you please watch Paul and Krista so Michael and I can go out for an hour or two after we have our breakfast?" I asked.

"My friend Heather gets paid for babysitting," Hanna said, looking a little sheepish.

"Well, okay, that's fair, how much do you charge for your services?" Michael asked.

"I don't know, Dad," Hanna said.

"You can't negotiate a contract without knowing what the endgame is, Sweetie," Michael said. "Here … come over here, I have a penny for you, that should be enough, right?"

"No!"

"Take a few minutes and decide what you want for your babysitting services. Then let me know what you need, and we'll try to strike a deal," he said. "You probably should do some research … so if you need a few minutes to make some calls or something … I'll wait."

Hanna and Michael hammered out an equitable price for her babysitting services, and a deal was struck, but it was five cents less than she asked.

"Toughen her up a bit," Michael said, "and it'll leave something on the table for her to go for."

"Michael," I said, "before we eat, maybe you should change. I just got those pants out of the cleaners."

Smiling over his glasses with those earthy green eyes of his, he said, "Okay, sweetie," and his eyes said, "I'm not angry anymore."

My eyes answered, "I still want the apartment date!"

I saw "Me too!" in his gaze.

Our eyes embrace and I hear a wailing sax somewhere in the distance, blowing jazz ... a syrupy interpretation served up by a tenor sax, sweet and hot. I close my eyes and listen. *Blow it baby,* I think, *blow it!*

The dice skitter away again, sizzling hot ... Bam! ... SEVENS! ... I win ... I win life's lottery ... Yes!

LaVergne, TN USA
08 December 2010

207800LV00003B/7/P